Awake In Hell

Helen Downing

ISBN: 10:1480009652
ISBN-13:978-1480009653

For:

Rev. William Downing

Marty Downing

Linda Lopreste

Patrick Haughey

With all my love.

ACKNOWLEDGMENTS

The amazing folks who gave me the opportunity to finally find the book hidden inside of me and get it out onto paper...

Michelle Vinson – Who was at the start and said "Keep going!"

Diana Welch –Colorized the cover art and gave me safe haven to finish the book.

Cathianne Porterfield – The greatest Editor ever.

Ryan Weber – Artist who created the cover.

Gabrielle Mappone - Photographer

1

Waking up in Hell is the worst part of my day. During sleep you can kind of forget where you are — dream about happy places, happier times — other than the heat, the oppressive heat that is always here. Because, what else would Hell be if not hot?

My bed is actually kind of comfortable. Well, more comfortable than anything else here. Sometimes I dream about when I was alive. Nothing major like working out life's big mysteries, but little moments like having an orgasm, or the look on my best friend Linda's face whenever I gave her relationship advice (something I am not qualified to do, by the way.) She would look at me with this intent admiration, as if no wisdom could be greater than mine. Dreams are the one thing Hell cannot take away from us. It is as if our creator is giving us one last peace despite our sins.

My alarm is set to go off exactly one hour before I want to get up. It's a psychic clock. We have a whole different set of tech down here.

Regardless, I wake up every morning with that sense of being more exhausted than I was when I went to bed. That's just one of the lovely amenities this place has to offer.

When I say amenities, please hear the facetious nature with which I proclaim such a thing. My "apartment" is about 8 feet by 8 feet. No TV, no phone, no air conditioner (obviously) and one window that does not open. The walls are gray, the floor is bare wood, and nothing is designed with comfort in mind. This is not my sanctuary, where I can escape Hell. It's my little corner of Hell that I get to call my own. I live in a relatively small building. I think there are about a dozen other tenants here, but we are not what you would call a friendly bunch, so I don't exactly know my neighbors. I rarely hear one of them. The occasional scream will seep through my walls, but that is pretty much it.

I hit the snooze button (which never works, yet I still try each morning) and I wake yawning and rubbing my sore, dry eyes against the super-heated air. I get dressed quickly, since I have little choice in my closet. It changes from day to day, but today is a prime example of what greets me each morning; a pair of shit-tan hip huggers a size too small (circa 1977) complimented by a blue polyester shirt with a lapel wider than the ass of a waitress at a greasy spoon. Additionally, I have been issued a g-string stained with some unknown substance. I cast t aside. Oh well, in keeping with the glass half-full mantra I've been employing lately, I think to myself, "beats yesterday's five layers of itchy underwear from the Victorian era." And if, by chance, today's outfit is worse than yesterday's, I simply look at the clothing of others and am eventually bound to see someone poor soul clearly worse off than myself. Indeed, as I look out my window right now, I spot someone across the street in an Eskimo coat and wool sweat pants. Who says the Devil doesn't have a sense of humor?

Ah, but it gets worse. Aside from the tortuous togs I must don for the day, there are other truths to face. One immediate concern — I need a job. I was fired three days ago from the job I've held ever since I found myself here. I can't say exactly when that was because there is no way to keep track of time in Hell. Although it is possible to make tally marks on the wall (one for every time you wake up) it seems futile and a bit of an annoyance. Things change down here all the time, with little or no warning. Like, for instance, my employment status.

I was in tech support at the IP&FW (Internet Porn and Fetish Web). See, we have high speed Internet down here but every search leads right to IP&FW. If you search for your grandmother's recipe for chocolate zucchini cake, you arrive at a site where naked girls sit and squirm on your granny's favorite dessert. If you attempt to look up your favorite football team, you land on overweight gay romance. Oh, and if this would have ever turned you on when you were alive, it will not down here. For instance if you search "hot lesbian sex," you'll be taken to images and videos of disfigured lesbians literally on fire, attempting to have sex. What can I say? This is Hell. I spent every day at a call center listening to newcomers bitch about not being able to follow their favorite sports teams or download a single Miley Cyrus mp3 from their computers. Then one day, I got a call from a gentleman who claimed that he couldn't get online at all. I asked him if he'd reset his modem and he didn't seem to know what I was talking about. I then asked him if he'd had Internet when he was breathing and he claimed that no, he was unable to get Internet access when he was among the living due to the fact that he lived in the woods and eschewed technology while he was alive. I pondered why he might want Internet now when he had gone so long without it. I imagined maybe he had more to entertain himself when he was alive; like HBO or masturbation. He claimed to have spent his entire welfare check every month on baked beans and guns. Oh, and the occasional purchase of lye and burlap bags for body disposal. Anyway, to make a long story short, I told him that he will occasionally have to reset his modem by unplugging it, waiting 30 seconds and plugging it back in — simple right? EVERYBODY knows that — right?

Well, he didn't and I told him exactly what to do step-by-step, which constitutes being helpful. Being helpful in tech support at IP&FW is in direct opposition to their primary directive, which is an immediate terminable offense. Fuck IP & fucking FW. How was I supposed to know that I was talking to the ONLY person in the entire Hell-verse that would find the resetting-the-modem spiel actually helpful?

So, now I have to find another job.

Here, there are no social services. You work for any of the small cottage businesses that pop up all the time, or you work for IP&FW, or you get stuck working for one of the big chain stores or a law firm. If you turn out to be totally unemployable, then you go work for the government — and the government of Hell is run by SATAN, I would assume (although

4

I can't say that I've ever met the guy personally). Trust me, no one goes to work for the government on purpose. With that in mind, I hit the streets telling myself I won't go home until I have secured employment somewhere.

I walk out and immediately have to adjust to the outside environment. Hell was created (I assume it was created at some point, as opposed to just sprouting up after the Fall) to look like any old city; standard grid streets, homeless people, tall buildings that seem to go up forever. There are a few random smaller buildings in between that seem to say the city was built up around them, although I think that is just part of the illusion. I mean, do you think Hell used to be a much nicer neighborhood with rising property values? No, me neither. There's an orange color to the atmosphere, like ambient light, making everything seem as if it's about to catch fire but never does. This is accompanied by the smell of phosphorous like someone behind you has just struck a match. All of this seems to magnify the hot and make it even hotter. People behave here just like they do in any city of the living, rushing around like absolutely everyone is late to something really important. The sidewalks and streets are worn and cracked and filled with potholes, but still usable. Every once in a while there will be a repair crew out to fix one, but I don't think it's to improve our infrastructure, I think it's because laying tar on a street in temperatures close to 200 degrees Fahrenheit in the shade sounds like a perfect job for someone in Hell. There is no sky here. If you try to seek the heavens whatever it is up there will burn your eyes and you will be blinded for a few minutes, like with a camera flash.

So, you have to be on your toes if you're going to stroll around in Hell.

There are three coffee shops within walking distance from my apartment. One makes weak, watery coffee strained through dirty socks, and one makes strong, bitter coffee strained through dirty socks. The last claims to be "organic" but the populace believes that they are serving the waste produced by people drinking the stuff at the other two shops. I'll need my caffeine boost today so I go for the strong, bitter choice. I walk past the hoard of beggars. Believe it or not the beggars are actually employed by the government to stand outside and beg from folks set to Hell. It's one of the more dead-end jobs you can have around here, no pun intended. I step inside and walk up to the counter. I'm third or fourth in line so I look at the bulletin board next to the cash register while I wait and see if any jobs are posted. They've the usual job fair notices from the chain stores, and one from (grrrrr) IP&FW, and a help-wanted sign for the coffee shop itself. So, I take a look behind the counter — could I do that for 12 to 14 hours a day? I shrug and commit to asking for an application when I get up there. Then I notice a small piece of paper tacked way up on the corner of the board. I can't really read it until I reach up and take it down. Then I see:

DO YOU BELONG HERE?

CALL US TO FIND OUT!

SECOND CHANCE TEMP AGENCY

(666)-573-2236

I look around and when I'm sure no one has noticed, I stick the note in my pocket.

2

Here comes the part you've been waiting for — the part where I tell you how I got here. See, the note that is now sitting quietly in my pocket is screaming in my mind. Do I belong here? I can't honestly say I know, without a doubt, that I deserved to go to Hell. I do know, however, that I didn't in any way, shape or form earn a ticket to Heaven either. I didn't do anything. And I don't mean that as an indignant "I was framed" kind of defense — I mean I *didn't do anything* with my time, with my talent, with my life. I was born Louise May Patterson. I had a normal childhood and a very nice set of parents, all things considered. I was in my mid-forties when I bit it, but I was still acting like a teenager. I lived at home with the aforementioned parents, or on the street, or with the occasional lover, always managing to never pay a single dime in rent, eat for free, and never reach the mentality of a true adult. I used to joke with Linda, back when she was still partying, that if I ever got a job she should shoot me in the head to put me out of my misery. We would laugh at all the "rats running the maze" every day — going to work at "o'dark thirty" in the morning to try and screw the other rats out of assistant manager of paper clip requisitions. Wake up, rush through a cup of coffee, spend nine to five at a job they all hated, go home and go to bed just to do it again the next day. That was never me, and never would have been me. I mean, really, what's the point?

So every day was a holiday for me and those in my circle at the time. This circle I speak of was always changing, my "lost boys and girls" — because everyone else grew up and left me. It didn't bother me much. They all thought they were smarter than me, and I knew I was smarter than all of them. I would move on just as they moved on. I'd take on the newly single, the addicts, the newcomers to town, the young ones... Occasionally I'd find a sugar daddy — usually a married one — to take me away from the small one-horse town where I grew up, and still lived.

But I always came back. It might have been the charm of my home town that drew me back, but I sincerely doubt it. More likely my adulterer and I just got bored with each other. I'd tell you the name of that town, where it is on a map, what great state it sits smack dab in the middle of, if it mattered. But it doesn't. Just suffice it to say, "it's a heap of shit filled with a bunch of smaller, less significant pieces of shit walking around in it." Believe me, if you lived there, you would wanna be wasted all the time too.

My only saving grace in that town was Linda. She was my bestie from the moment we met. We were 19 years old and she was living with a group of guys who were dealing blow in the club where I hung out, and I was one of their best customers. The night they finally invited me back to their place I had the adult version of sugar plum dreams. I had visions of being gang-banged and free coke dancing in my head. When I got there and saw her lying back on the sofa while some random guy was cutting a line on her stomach my heart lurched. Whoa, I've finally found a cosmic sister! She looked me right in the eye and gave me a dreamy smile — she had a barely noticeable overbite unless (as I came to learn later) she was giving you her "this is my dreamy smile" face. It's a surprisingly effective face... then she scowled at Len (the leader of this particular pack) and said "Who's the new bitch?"

I actually let out a small squeal, like I did as a kid whenever I opened up the Christmas gift that I'd been wading through socks, underwear, and school supplies to get to. That night there was no orgy — there was no sex at all. It was just me and Linda — up all night jazzed up on cocaine and letting every detail of our lives spill out all over each other like an overflowing milkshake. Indeed, I stained her with my strawberry, and her chocolate is still imprinted on me. We talked faster than the speed of light until our voices were hoarse and the boys had given up all hope of getting laid. By morning we knew everything about one another. I still remember watching the sun coming up and actually feeling different. Like today I was new, because today I had a friend who was going to change my life. I guess that is kinda like how falling in love would have felt — if I'd ever fallen in love. But for me it was always Linda. From that point on I didn't need to fall in love, or get a job, or buy a house... as long as I had Linda, I was complete.

I know what you're probably thinking. That I died of a drug overdose or an accident involving drunk driving or something. Well, neener neener neener — NOTHING like that. In fact, my death was sort of valiant. I died of breast cancer, which, by the way, pisses me off beyond all reason. I was never very good about going to the doctor. First of all, I hated the fact that you had to have a blood test or a pee test and I'm sure they test for drugs even if they say they don't. And I know that hippopotamus thingy is supposed to protect you, but I OBVIOUSLY have a problem trusting people in authority positions, so I never really bought that either. I really hardly ever got sick anyway. Besides it's not like I just had a Blue Cross/Blue Shield card hanging out of my purse, so one trip to the emergency room would mean avoiding calls from bill collectors for at least 6 months after. That was all more trouble than it's worth, so the only preventative care I took of my breasts was the fact that every other guy in the tri-county area had felt me up or had them in his mouth. Don't you think at least ONE of those guys would have told me if he felt a lump? Nope. So by the time I noticed it (I never claimed to be the sharpest tool in the drawer, ya know) it was full blown Stage 4 "bend-over-and-kiss-your-ass-goodbye" cancer.

There were some good things about it. It was the first and only time anyone other than Linda called me "brave." I went from junkie-whore to hero. Everyone kept looking at me with tears building up in their eyes and they'd say some greeting card platitude bullshit like "everything happens for a reason" or "the One above works in mysterious ways" — as if that would make me feel better. But then they'd all say the word "BRAVE." I was hardly signing up to be the new Buffy or running into a burning building or anything. It wasn't like I had a choice — dying of old age in my sleep or getting murdered very slowly in front of the whole town by an invisible killer and I couldn't protect myself or stop it from happening. It's truly weird how having cancer, a disease that's not contagious or discriminative, all of a sudden makes someone a good person.

I use the term junkie whore loosely, and mostly out of jest. I was never really a junkie, in the real sense of the word. Sure, I did plenty of drugs and even more men, but I was never paid to have sex. I never crawled around on my knees searching for a crack rock. I never stuck a needle full of heroin into my arm. I guess you could say I was classier than your average party slut. That's a better term, not "junkie whore," rather, "party slut." I always looked amazing, had beautiful skin and great legs and a kick-ass wardrobe. And the greatest asset I'd ever been given, I would assume by a higher power, but since getting here I can't say that definitively, was my rack. I had the tits of a 25 year old even after I'd hit the big 4-0. You know the pencil test? The one where you take a pencil and put it under your boob and let go of it, and if it stays put then it's time to see a plastic surgeon? My D-cups were still dropping pencils on the last day they were on earth. This, by the way, preceded my last day on earth by seven and a half months.

After my initial diagnosis everything just sorta slowed down for me. Not because I was immobilized by being sick, but I felt the need to take a step back and become an observer in my own life. I remember reading the occasional book or article in a magazine, or seeing someone on Oprah or the Today Show who said that it took finding out that they were going to die before they started living in the moment. It was just the opposite for me. I had always lived in the moment. Figuring the future would work itself out, or maybe on some level I always knew I didn't have a future. Living in the now is fast, because a moment is gone the instant it arrives. So to truly live in the moment is to be a bit crazed, a little manic, a frenzied, harried, hapless person who, like the Fool in the tarot deck, is walking blindly toward a cliff with a smile and a song. This was much different. The day that I went into the doctor's office and sat down, playing with my prosthetic bra so that I could scratch the scars underneath without it being too noticeable, and the doctor told my mom that she might want to wait outside while he discussed some important new information with me privately...everything just kinda paused. The universe took a deep breath, drew back, and punched me right in the gut.

From the moment the doctor said "Terminal" to me, I never ever caught my breath again.

From that point on everything started moving frame by frame. I could finally stop and see my surroundings. I could hear my own heartbeat. I could smell the fear in everyone around me. I wasn't living for the moment anymore, I was trying to survive it. That's a whole different kettle of fish.

So anyway, that's how I died, and I do not recommend it. I suggest that if you are shopping for a way to die, pick during a nap when you're old and gray or something tragic and sudden like getting hit by a train or spontaneous combustion. But of course, very few of us get a chance to pick how to shuffle off the mortal coil. Speaking of choosing how you die, the whole "suicide guarantees you a ticket to the lake of fire" myth? Is just that — a myth. From what I understand, everyone that ends up here is here because of how they lived, not how they died. Oh, and I haven't seen anything that looks even remotely like a lake since I got here. Just a little piece of FYI to make the price of admission worthwhile.

3

Alright, so I said I would not go home until I had secured employment somewhere. However, this is, quite literally, Hell and job hunting sucks ass in the best of circumstances, so it stands to be concluded that down here it is outright torture. It's not even noon yet and I'm already over it. I stood at the counter and filled out an application at all 3 coffee shops, primarily because I wanted to go check the bulletin boards at the other two shops for one of those temp agency slips. The other two did not have one on their boards, which leads me to believe that the one that was on mine might be old. Hopefully they still have some placements left. I look into the distant skyline and see the government buildings where just the commute itself would take up half my day. Then I turn around and look behind me at the mammoth chain stores, filled with discount crap that usually falls apart from the strain of taking it out of its packaging. I can't work at these places. Especially now that I know that there might be some sort of redemption clause that I hadn't heard about before. How can anyone sit in front of a luncheonette that serves cat food on toast with a small tin cup begging from people who didn't give a damn about humankind when they were alive after they find out that there might be a remote chance of getting out of here? But, since openings at a place like that has got to go as soon as they are vacant, and since there's always way more people in Hell than jobs, I'm starting to sweat for reasons other than the temperature outside. Good jobs are always at a premium. I mean, that's part of the problem with working in the afterlife -- no one retires, and no one dies, and no one moves....at least not anyone I've ever met.

Not that I've met a whole lot of people here.

Quite frankly, despite my incredibly full social calendar in life...I've been a bit of a wallflower in death. I haven't adjusted well. Even though I'm pretty sure (like I said, time means nothing here, especially when you're facing eternity...) that I've been here for a while. And I'm sorry, but does it matter if I've been here for a year or 100 years? I can take my sweet old time to get used to the idea that I was apparently such a turd-monkey that I warranted going straight to Hell for the rest of time itself!

When I first got here I thought I was still alive. See, I don't remember the actual act of dying. I remember the whole cancer thing, and I remember my Mom and Dad at the kitchen table with Power of Attorney papers and other legal shit that they kept shoving in front of me and I kept signing. They could have handed me a million dollar check and I'd have just signed it and pushed it back across the table to them at that point. I was still numb.

I remember the Doctor saying that my cancer has metastasized despite the mastectomy and had now invaded several lymph nodes and a few other required organs. He said I had six months to a year, and I remember the day that marked the 6 month anniversary of that meeting. I don't remember what we did, but I do remember going to bed that night thinking "From this point on I'm on borrowed time."

I remember lying in a hospital bed surrounded by people. I can't really remember who was there, and I find it fascinating that my mind has the impression that there were a lot of people around me. I mean, how many people are you planning to have at your death bed? Even today I'm thinking three people tops, and I was young and quite popular (if I do say so myself). Yet my cloudy brain won't show me faces but gives me the impression that there were more. I see my Mom standing over me, and she's talking but I can't hear what she says, then "fade to black", as the movie people say.

And, sorry if this part ruins some great fantasy, but there was no tunnel, or doorway, or bright light. There was no floating above my body or watching my own funeral. There was no giant pearly gates (for obvious reasons), nor was there a trial, a judgment, or a sentence. Just dark and quiet for a while, then I woke up here. Not in my apartment, though. I woke up under an overpass outside of town. I had to walk for what seemed like forever and the whole time I was thinking "who in the fuck lets a dying girl fall asleep outside on the side of a road?"

What's weird is that I can remember every single detail of some random Saturday when I was 20 years old, and I can remember every single gift I received for my 30th birthday. I know that I was 43 years old when I died, but I can't remember turning 43. It seems the closer I got to my doom the more my brain started to purge important details. Either that or I had successfully killed enough brain cells at that point to be legally retarded.

Once I reached town I knew I wasn't in Kansas (or any other state) anymore. There were huge skyscrapers, and it was all glass, and the heat was intolerable. And everyone around me looked like they were leaving or on their way to the worst costume party ever thrown. I walked until I was about to buckle from heat stroke (or so I thought... again, still thinking I'm alive...) that's when I came upon the gargantuan IP&FW building. I looked across the street and the opposing glass facade reflected the entire IP&FW building, so much so that it obscured the reflective building's identity. I entered the officious building — and was offered employment — after being told I was dead.

Oh yeah, and after that they let me in on that I was naked and issued me a mohair spa robe infested with body lice.

Funny enough, they never actually had to tell me where I was. Even the dullest knife in my mother's entire baby-proofed kitchen would have figured that one out.

So, I have no idea how crowded the church was when they laid me to rest. I will never know if Matt, the guy that once kidnapped me and held me hostage in his house for three days begging me to marry him showed up. Or my high school sweetheart Bo, who once took a possession rap for me when we were caught smoking weed behind the gym and yelled "WAIT FOR ME, DARLING! NO MATTER HOW LONG IT TAKES!" as they were carting him off to Juvey. He was only there for like twelve hours and when he got out there was a line of little gangster groupies waiting to suck his dick, so other than the occasional Christmas card in later years, I never heard from him again. That was the first of a long line of men in my life who never learned how to turn down strange.

Anyway, back to the funeral. See, I'm lying in bed, totally nude since the heat is so oppressive I can't even stand a sheet on me, and even if the magic closet provided pajamas who would want to wear them? I don't care what anyone from Nevada, or New Mexico, or Florida says...you can't get used to the heat when it's 198 degrees outside. But, lying in bed, naked as a jaybird, covered in sweat, smack dab in the middle of Hell is NOT the place to start reminiscing about men, so I had to cut the whole "hall of fame" thinking short. See, masturbation is not possible down here. I don't know what they do to us; drug our food, lobotomize us while we are in the void, or maybe it's because our bodies aren't real...they are just constructs our minds create so that we can walk around and touch stuff. But some things, you can't touch... not effectively anyway.

So I spend most evenings waiting for sleep to overcome me by imagining my funeral one more time. Sometimes it's in a church, sometimes by the gravesite, sometimes it's weird and futuristic and I'm in a spaceship airlock getting jettisoned into the starry night. Once I imagined a funeral pyre and every asshole that ever walked out on me was forced to throw his ass on it. Now *that* was a great funeral.

In reality, I'm sure my parents did a quiet service at the local Methodist church, where they were members and I was not. The ladies auxiliary down at the fire hall probably made fried chicken and the Methodist women brought cucumbers and onions, and ambrosia, and green bean casserole. My dad always said that Methodists believe you can't get into heaven unless you bring a covered dish. Maybe that was it, maybe if I'd just shredded a few carrots into some lime jello I'd be playing poker with St. Peter right now. But I don't think it's really that simple.

I'm sure my mom cried buckets of tears at the service. Rev. Dawson used his solemn voice, and told a few stories that sounded very personal like we were old buddies. Then he'd tell a few lies, about what a good heart I had and how much I loved Jesus and now I was dancing with angels. My dad might have even shed a tear at that reference, since it would have reminded him of my 4th grade dance recital. I was supposed to skip across the stage behind Mary Conway but Mary stopped short because she was so nervous she thought she was gonna throw up. So I ran into her and she turned around and was facing me with a greenish look on her face and I screamed to the top of my lungs "Don't you dare puke on me bitch!" My mom was mortified. Mary was so stunned that she turned and ran off the stage. The principal was scowling while other parents were mumbling under their breath...and in the middle of it all was my Dad...laughing his ass off. To this day, every time anyone says anything about not feeling well or dancing, my dad has the same retort. "Don't you dare puke on me bitch!" followed by gales of laughter. My mom does the "my-husband-is-a-doofus" eye roll so much whenever he does that bit that she starts to resemble an Armand Marseille doll.

Linda and Hank were surely sitting with Mom and Dad. Hank is Linda's husband, and the source of every major fight Linda and I have ever had where drugs and alcohol was not involved. But to be honest, Hank is a nice enough guy and he was probably very handy to have around, what with all the blubbering and stuff. I can't see Hank crying over my death, not that we didn't like each other well enough, but Hank is probably the only person in my life who could see the bright side to my dying. I don't think he was dancing on my grave, mind you... but he probably was not inconsolable either. Linda and I, on the other hand, have not gone a single day since we were 19-years-old without talking, at least on the phone. Of course, by now she's probably used to the fact that I'm gone, and who knows? Maybe she even has a new best friend. But on the day of my funeral, which is every day for me, Linda is still sobbing over my grave and putting a flower on my casket.

Suddenly, I get a flash of a face very quickly in my mind. It's a man. Is he handsome? Is he angry? Concerned? I try to grab onto it, try to focus in on him, who he is, but then it's gone. Like when you hear a car go by and for a split second you hear their radio blasting a song that you love, and you realize that even though the car has been passed for several minutes the song is still going on in your head. It was weird, like a memory, but not. Like something familiar, but new. It filled me with a sense of panic and, strangely enough, a pang of longing. My construct of a heart starts beating faster, and I suddenly have the urge to either laugh or cry, and I won't know which until it starts.

Maybe I should stop thinking now. Since my mind is creating men from thin air, and my fake body is obviously reacting, it's probably best to just try and get some sleep.

Tonight there are no happy dreams, like of Linda and I driving down a highway in her Mustang – windows down and the radio blaring something that we'd be humiliated if anyone we knew caught us listening to (read: Air Supply or REO Speedwagon). Tonight my dreams were directed by Andy Warhol— all existential and hard to follow.

There's this adorable blond child, a little girl with ringlets stepping straight out of a 1940's casting room. She's wearing a blue taffeta dress that has a sash with flowers on it, Blue Bells I think they are called? She's running away from me in patent leather mary-janes. But she stops every few feet to let me catch up, giggling her adorable little girl giggle, so we're obviously playing a game.

Suddenly I look to my left and there's a bush with tiny flowers on it that are exactly like the ones on the girls sash. I walk over to get a closer look, maybe try and catch the scent of the flowers. Under the bush is a pastel blue egg. But it doesn't belong there. It wasn't put there by the bird who laid it. It's an Easter egg! We are at an Easter Egg Hunt! I look for the little girl and now she's carrying a basket with several other colored eggs in it. "Look" I say, "Here's one!"

She bounces over and picks it up, placing it gently in her basket. Then she looks at me and gives me the cutest little kid scowl and says "Stop helping me!" I laugh and say "Okay, I'm sorry."

Suddenly, we are in the hospital where I passed away. I feel the heavy starched sheets under my hands, and I smell that horrible antiseptic hospital smell. She is by my bed, still in her Easter dress. She looks at me and says "Answer the phone, Louise."

"What phone?" I respond groggily

Now she's making a phone noise.

"What?" I'm confused.

Every time she opens her mouth now, it rings like an antique phone.

I open my eyes and realize I've been dreaming. I also suddenly discover that my face is wet. Why was I crying in my sleep? I try to remember, to hold onto the image of the sweet little girl, but it's so hard to keep anything in my head with that incessant ringing. The dream begins to fade away, and I try to mentally chase it, but...

I reach over to hit the snooze button, my daily dose of futility. But the alarm is not going off. Yet still, there's that noise, that fucking RINGING!

I sit up and start to look around. It doesn't take long to take in the entire apartment. It's what the living would call, "an efficiency." It's basically the size of a cubicle in an airport restroom. It's got a sink with a shelf over it for the single dish, single bowl, and single glass I own. I'm not planning on hosting a dinner party any time soon so why bother with more? There's an oven that I've never turned on, and if you have to ask why you've obviously not been paying attention. It also boasts a miserably small bathroom with room for a toilet and a standing-room-only shower that sprays no hot water, yet no cold water. All you get is sort of tepid. And don't even get me started on the water pressure.

And then, there's the *closet* — room for one outfit that will appear each day. After all those luxuries, there's enough room left for a small desk (for the computer and the alarm clock), a broken chair, and my bed. I've never had a phone here. First of all, who would call me? I'm dead. Not to mention that I've worked in a call center since I got to this shithole so why would I want a phone anywhere near me when I'm not at work? And third ...

Wait...

I stand up and walk to the far wall of my apartment with my mouth hanging open like a goldfish. "agape" is the word I think for this expression.   There's   a   mother   fuckin'   PHONE   on   the   wall. Why is this a surprise to me? After all this time (however long it's been) I should know that this kind of bullshit supernatural magic crap happens. I should be nonchalant about the fact that all of the sudden there's a telephone, a really old telephone, with the horn receiver hanging off the side kind of telephone, ringing it's ass off in the middle of my apartment. But what can I say? I'm stunned. I just keep staring at it, like it's going to jump off the wall and bite me. It doesn't.

It just keeps ringing.

And ringing.

Finally my left temporal lobe decides to join the party. Motor skills? Present. Clarity of thought? Accounted for. One of you guys want to reach up and grab the DAMNABLE PHONE? Thank you.

"Hello?" I say, cautiously.

"Hello. This is Second Chance Temp Agency!" says an incredibly cheerful female operator. "Calling to remind Louise Patterson that her appointment with us starts in exactly 22 minutes." Her voice is so perfect it almost sounds recorded.

"Okay." I croak in response, "But..."

"There will be a cab waiting for you outside your apartment in approximately 9 minutes."

"Yeah, but...."

"Please hurry Louise. You don't want to be late for your very first appointment." I swear you can HEAR her smiling.

"Okay, but…"

"Bye now! See you in 22, no wait…21 minutes!"

Dead air. She hung up. So I yell into the ether through the antique mouthpiece…

"BUT I HAVEN'T PUT IN AN APPLICATION YET! HOW DID YOU KNOW I GOT THE NOTICE??"

I let the receiver fall out of my hand where it swings by its cord against the wall. I figure if there's anyone else out there who wants to call me it really doesn't matter whether or not the device is hung properly.

I go to my closet and waiting there is an absolutely ridiculous adult size taffeta pastel blue dress with a flowery sash. The kind of dress a soccer mom would buy for her 7-year old daughter to wear on picture day or to church. What are those little blue flowers called? Pansies, maybe? For some reason, it looks familiar to me, and makes me kind of sad. But for the life of me, I can't remember where I've seen such a goofy dress. I pull it over my head and smooth out the ruffles slipping on the matching patent leather mary-janes. I grimace as I put them on. Today promises to be a weird day. Even for Hell.

4

Thanks to the fact that everyone sweats profusely down here, make-up is pointless. They do sell it at the chain stores, and the women who work there put layers and layers of it on their faces, I think out of sheer boredom, since they can go hours without a customer most of the time. So, when you see someone walking down the street looking like a cross between a deranged clown and hooker who's been pummelled in the face by several johns and her pimp, you know exactly how she spends her day. Or, you can at least narrow it down to three ways: deranged clown, abused hooker, or most likely working at a chain store.

The chain stores are enormous. Unlike the high-rise mirrored front downtown buildings which are TALL (so I would assume. I've never seen the top of one of them.), the chain stores are just big. They sprawl out all over the edge of the city. Like the big chain stores from the living world the front of the stores is taken up by miles of concrete divided by yellow lines to depict parking spaces with an occasional one being used as a corral for shopping carts. And yes, in Hell every shopping cart has the little wheel that is askew so the cart is constantly veering left. Some things are just a given down here.

But unlike the stores in the breathing world, these stores are ghost towns on the inside. Most of us never go in after we've been here long enough to know better. However, if you occasionally find yourself in need of something, or if you've recently fallen and bumped your head, then you may find yourself inside a chain store. The people who work there are worse than the call center people at IP&FW. If you ask them where something is they will give you directions to the opposite side of the store. That is if you get their attention. Most likely, when you walk up to one of them they will be "busy" reading a magazine or applying yet another layer of make-up on their hideous faces. Here's the bizarre thing — just another one of those things that make you realize exactly where you are — no matter how empty the store seems to be, it will be packed when you want to check out. Everyone will decide to check out at the exact same time. That's the magic of truly being damned.

Anyway, today I'm grateful for the no make-up thing, since I would have been tempted to put little circles of blush on my cheeks with little eyeliner freckles on top. That is how horrid this outfit is. I'm trying to decide if I should be quoting Bette Davis from *Whatever Happened to Baby Jane?* or Do-Se-Do'ing with a guy in a 10-gallon hat and sparkly cowboy boots when my cab pulls up. The driver hangs out the window and says "Lou-weeze Patterson?" Then he responds to my nod with a jerk of his head and barks, "get in, I got 13 minutes to get you downtown."

Now, normally I never, EVER, take cabs in Hell. Why, you ask? Well, you would ask if you were born and raised in the middle of America where livestock outnumbers people 5 to 1 and everyone is *nice*. However, anyone who lived in an inner-city-type environment? Yeah, you get the idea, just take the worst cab driver ever and multiply those skills by a factor of a hundred and twenty seven — squared. The only time you ever hear anyone praying in Hell is when they're locked in the back of a cab racing down the wrong street and headed in the opposite direction of their destination, while a cabbie who's steering with one finger, looking directly BEHIND him hawking beenie babies, super vitamins, and pirated DVDs to his fares. That is why I don't just jump right into the backseat the minute the driver comes to a — thankfully—full stop.

"I was actually thinking of walking. Can you give me the address for the temp agency?" I say, trying to sound casual, like 'Hey, it's a lovely day down here in Hell, perfect for a nine mile walk in a dress that makes me look like Shirley Temple on crack!'

But the cabbie just chuckles and says "Not today Ms. Patterson. I have a special tag. I'm cleared to take you straight to the agency."

I have no idea what that means, but for some reason I trust that it must mean that he's okay. So I hop in the backseat, sort of wrap the frayed seat belt around me for a false sense of safety, and say "Let's go, then!"

It takes 11 minutes before he pulls up to the biggest, shiniest building I've seen yet. I'm ashamed to say that I'm actually feeling nervous. Okay, maybe a little scared. Alright, close to booting all over the sidewalk kind of terrified. Why? Then it hit me. I'm 43 years old, and I might have been 43 for a few years now. And, fuck me running, but this would constitute my first ever job interview. I not only have no skills, but I have no experience in bullshitting people to make them think that I might have some skills. I'm screwed! I try to turn around and jump back into the cab, but the driver just laughs and guns it. I get a lung full of burned rubber as he drives away. So, I take a deep breath, smooth out my ruffles once more, and head inside. How hard can it be to do a temp job anyway? Right?

5

At IP&FW everyone worked on the first three floors. The building was obviously a high-rise, and so there had to be many stories above us, but no one ever went up there. In fact, the elevators only went up to number 3. Not that you could take the elevator, since it was always out of order, but we all had our turn of trying to duck under the caution tape and giving it a try. I once walked up the additional flight of stairs to the fourth floor, but the doors were all bolted, so no entry that way either. I remember thinking that this was the one thing that didn't make sense, since it would have been much more tortuous for us if we'd had to walk up 17 or 18 flights of stairs instead of just 2 or 3. I guess part of being sent to Hell is that nothing is supposed to make sense to you ever again.

And that's the other thing. Everything down here is dirty, and with the orangy light it looks even dingier except for the giant buildings, which are always gleaming. The outside of this building is so sparkling that I can barely look at it. How do they keep it that clean? Someone has to be on one of those pulley cart things 24/7 with a super squeegee and a lifetime supply of windex to keep just one of these buildings in this condition. Yet, I've never seen anyone on a pulley cart thing. Not once. Of course, I can't really see all the way to the top of the buildings, because of the whole fuck-up-your-eyes-whenever-you-look-up situation. Anyway, that was what I was thinking when I walked into the lobby of the agency. So I was distracted. So I didn't hear when a guy started calling my name.

"Louise!"

"Louise Patterson!"

"Louise?"

"Last call for Louise Patterson?"

Then this really young guy with a sweet face and a slight build, which happened to be dressed like a monkey on an organ grinder steps back into the elevator and says "Another no show. Man, the folks down here really are a bunch of head cases..."

Wait. Did he just say my name? Why did he say "down here"? Did he just call me a head case?

"WAIT!" I yell as the elevator doors begin to close. "I'm Louise Pat..."

The doors shut. 'Great job dumbass.' I think to myself. 'You made it as far as the lobby.' That was what I was *thinking*. But while I was thinking that, I was apparently *yelling* this:

"FUCK FUCK FUCKITY FUCK!"

And I was only halfway through this particular expletive escapade when the elevator doors re-opened.
There was monkey suit boy staring at me with a bemused look on his face. "Well then, step on up for the ride of your life Ms. Patterson!"

Now I'm really about to hurl. I've fucked this up 7 ways from bloody Sunday and I haven't even gotten to the office yet. So, I decide to use the one skill I happen to have...the skill of seduction. I check my reflection in the elevator doors and start swishing my hair around, and open my eyes really wide, trying to make them look more doe-ish.

"So, obviously you know my name, what's yours?" I ask in my sweetest tone.

"I'm called Will, m'am" He really is just adorable, with big brown eyes hiding underneath a mop of dirty blond hair. I would describe him as middle-America average, but I'm sure there are some girls in the small town he grew up in who are still dreaming of him.

"Oh Will..." I say giggling like a schoolgirl, "Don't call me M'am, it makes me feel like I should ask you if your Mom is home!" Giggle giggle... damn this is hard when you're on the verge of a total panic attack.

Will, the Monkey Suit Boy looked at me and started to laugh! That's a first for me, and not a pleasant one. Most men on earth would be panting by this time, if not out of sincere interest, at least because an obviously-easy, hot girl targeted him for some reason and he's about to have a heart attack.

"Okay, Louise" Will, the monkey-boy, says with a hint of condescension, "First, Will is not short for "Willing." And second, don't worry, I'm not going to tell the boss that you attempted to implode our lobby with F-bombs, okay?" he laughs in a conspiratorial way.

Relief. "Thanks Will." Okay, so Will is a bit of a dick, but at this point I'll take it. "You don't have a Xanax on you, do you Will?" I ask, only kind-of kidding.

"Nope. But drugs don't work here anyway, so you're just gonna have to shove the stuffing back in, zip up, and... here we are! Floor 37— welcome to the agency, Louise."

I'm on the 37th floor? Now my panic attack is accompanied by a weird sense of vertigo. How long has it been since I've been this far up in the air? I can't remember. Partially because I don't know how long I've been dead and partially because of my Swiss cheese memory from when I was alive. I give Will the Monkey Boy a weak smile and edge out of the elevator along the wall. I'm suddenly feeling very acrophobic. If I were actually breathing I would have fainted by now. I cling to the wall on the far side of the office and look across what seems like miles and miles of sky blue carpet at a woman standing behind a counter holding a clipboard. She's looking at me expectantly with a Vanna-White smile plastered on her face. I think she's the phone chick.

"Ms. Patterson! So happy you made it... glances at her watch... finally." Yep, that's her.

"Sorry," I say with just a touch of my panic sticken *inside-my-head* voice bleeding through, "there was some confusion in the lobby."

I'm creeping along as I'm talking — like this is totally normal behavior for someone who is trying to get a job. I wonder for a minute about how many folks are interviewing today, how many other pathetic Hellions are hoping that they can get a real "second chance" from The Second Chance Temp Agency. Then I wonder, for just a moment, about how ridiculous I really am compared to everyone else they've seen, today or any day. I get to a window and freeze. Holy shit, Can I look outside and see Hell from 37 stories above? I look and see nothing, and then I turn my head back to the reception area and still see nothing. Dammit, now I have to negotiate my way to Vanna totally blind. Then it suddenly occurs to me, that I am the most ridiculous person I've ever seen, so I'm probably a total freak show to everybody here. "Like Lady Gaga in a nunnery." I say under my breath, as I keep on feeling for the wall, now for the added reason of not being able to see combined with the overwhelming fear of falling through the floor.

"It's just me and Will who've seen your reaction Louise." says Vanna. "And, you'll be pleased to know that you are our only appointment today."

Can she read my mind???

"Yes." she says with a grin that I still can't see but is obviously there. "And, while you are the only appointment today I feel I must remind you that you're now 7 minutes late for your very first meeting."

You know, for a woman who is facing eternity, this bitch sure gets all worked up over the concept of time. Crap, she probably heard that. I'm going to have to watch what I think as well as what I say around here, what with Vanna-the-ever-cheerful-receptionist inside my head.

"My name is Gabby, Louise. And open your eyes. You can see now."

I open my eyes and to my dismay I've not made it as far as I thought. I'm still about 50 feet away from the reception desk, and there doesn't seem to be any other way to get to it but to walk across the room. So I take a deep breath and take a step forward. Then I panic again. Then I fall to my knees and start crawling. Yep, I'm *crawling* to Gabby. This job is in the bag, don't you think?

I finally make it to the counter and pull myself up as if I'm hanging off a ledge. "I'm sorry." I say with a shaky voice "I'm just not used to being so high... well, far up I mean."

Why did I feel the need to establish that? Like maybe she would think I was under the influence? It's like Will said, drugs don't work here anyway.

Okay, so when I was breathing, I was kind of smart. "Kind of" because I was great at puzzles, very quick on my feet with a joke, had an awesome memory, tested well... you know, that kind of smart. But I was also incredibly, mind-numbingly, stubbornly stupid sometimes. I remember reading on a bathroom wall once "A wise man learns from others, a fool must learn from experience." I remember digging through my purse for a pen so that I could scratch "I'm a fool then!" proudly under it. I believed in the school of hard knocks. I thought whoever tells me not to do shit that they did — then turn around and talk about a person being the sum of all their experience — is either a fucking hypocrite or assumes that I'm an idiot, requiring spoon feeding instead of being free to have the same "growth" experiences they had. And I talked. A lot. Way too much. I talked and talked and talked about what I was doing, who I was doing it to, and I talked to the wrong people. There were times when my mother would just about have her illusion set, convincing herself that I'd been out all night just hanging with Linda, having a "girl's night out", just a couple of kids blowing off steam; until I would stumble in and start telling her gory details about the latest party, the latest lay, the latest boutique drug. I wasn't trying to hurt her, I was just so incredibly stupid that I thought by telling her all of that she would know that I was smart enough to handle it. Even when she was in tears, I still kept talking. Somewhere, in my muddled brain, I believed that I was convincing her that I was too cool to get damaged. That I was immune to the problems of others like me. Yeah, I was that kind of fucking stupid.

"Louise." I look up and see Gabby looking at me with almost sad eyes. Her too-wide grin was replaced with a tender smile. I silently cursed myself once more for allowing my thoughts to wander to something that personal with a telepath around. And how interesting is it that down here the prospect of a telepathic receptionist in a temp agency is only mildly alarming? Instead of continuing to reveal anymore secrets I looked over the counter to see what kind of not-really-funny joke her closet had pulled on her this morning. She was wearing an old fashioned A-line dress. The kind Doris Day would have worn in the 1950's. Not exactly the height of fashion, but not really horrible either. "How do you...?" I started to ask her when she began hurrying around the counter toward me.

"As I was starting to explain..." she launched, "you are not the first person to have that reaction when they come here for the first time. In fact, we have these patches to help you with the vertigo." She waved a small flesh-colored sticker at me. The grin was back.

"Are you allowed to do that?" I ask, somewhat surprised. "You know, to make people... comfortable?"

Gabby came the rest of the way from behind her counter and walked toward me. She was so graceful she seemed to float over instead of walk. I was reminded of those old moldy movies my mom used to love — the ones that were all black & white both literally and figuratively. And the women were perfect, with tiny waists and pointy boobs, and all the kisses were closed mouth and looked like they should hurt, and people fell in love after one dinner date and then lived happily after ever. Gabby looked like one of those women, even her face up close looked like it was photographed, then airbrushed, then photo-shopped back onto her head. She was tall for a woman, about 5'8" and statuesque, which is a fancy word for thin but with nice tits and good hips. She was probably quite stunning when she was alive. With her beauty and fit body she appeared ageless, like she could pass for 30 or 60 and get away with either one. My face started to burn as I realized that she may have well heard all those thoughts as she glided to my side and gave me a slight, secretive smile, as if we were old girlfriends sharing an inside joke. "I'll tell you what Louise, I won't tell the boss if you don't." Then she reached over, took my hand, turned it over, and placed the small patch over my forearm.

I felt better immediately. I mean REALLY better. Not just no longer dizzy, or gripped with fear, but I felt lighter too, like maybe I could glide now, like Gabby. All my anxiety about the job interview was gone, and I almost... well... I almost felt giddy. I felt like laughing. And I realized that very moment that I hadn't laughed, really laughed since I was alive. Then that kind of made me sad for a minute, but it was only a minute and then I felt good again. It was a whirlwind of emotions, a sensation kind of like being high, but with more euphoria, and less nausea.

"Wow, that's an awesome patch!" I said to Gabby, who laughed out loud in response. "Here's another little pleasure I can offer, if you think you can manage it. How about a cup of coffee?"

"Sure." I answered with my newly chipper voice. Oh fuck, maybe I've drunk the proverbial Kool-Aid and am about to become a grinner! "Unless it's from the organic place, then never mind."

"Oh no! This is my coffee! I brew it myself. How do you take it?"

"I like my coffee like I like my men. Strong, tan, and artificially sweet." That line always got a laugh when I was breathing. Gabby didn't. But she did give me one of those "oh-you're-so-silly" half grins. Suddenly there was the sound of a door being swung open. I mean swung open. I could actually feel a small breeze from the direction of the door. And from behind it a loud booming voice with a sharp clipped accent bellows "Oi, Gabby! I assume Ms. Patterson has been through the orientation process? I would think, given the amount of time she's been out there that she's not only oriented, but quite possibly fully trained to do YOUR job!" It was loud, but it wasn't mean. He didn't sound grumpy at all. Maybe a little exasperated, but his voice was filled with humor. I pictured an old man with a beard, like Santa Claus, only from Ireland or Scotland or somewhere. Gabby was not the least bit bothered by all of the yelling. She just walked, or glided, over to me with a steaming cup of coffee that looked and smelled better than anything I've ever seen down here. I gave myself just one more second to breathe it in and take the first glorious sip.

"So, time to bite the bullet?" I ask with just a bit of the old trepidation back for an encore.

"Yes, it's time for you to meet the boss." Gabby was back to her old grinning self.

"Thanks Gabby, for the coffee and for the patch." I said, with sincere gratitude.

"No problem. Good luck, Louise." she answered as she ushered me into the corridor.

With just my thoughts, because I knew she was still reading me, I relayed one more message...

'Even though, as you know, I'm not stupid. I know what an adhesive bandage looks like, and I know I started to feel better the second you touched me.'

I could hear Gabby laughing out loud again as I approached the open door that would change my life... or death... whatever.

6

Human touch is very rare in Hell. I remember when I was at IP&FW there were a few in the call center who tried to date, but it never really worked out. First of all, there's no real age or aging down here. People just show up, usually the same age when they died, because I guess that when we die we approximate ourselves through memory. I really don't know, but I do know that no one ages once they get here. If they show up young, then they stay young. If they show up old, then... well, you get it. So anyway, there's no way to know just how big of an age difference there is. You may look the same age, but one of you may have been here for a hundred years while the other just arrived yesterday. Makes for bizarre dinner conversation. The only thing I could compare it to in the world would be a just spurned divorcee having dinner with a confirmed bachelor. She's all sobbing and screaming while he looks bored and asks for the check. And you haven't seen sobbing and screaming until you see someone eternally damned who is sobbing and screaming. And of course there's no possibility of getting lucky after a date in Hell. Fucking is as futile as masturbation. You can work at it for hours but it will never come to fruition. Most likely more of you than not know that feeling, right? We've all been there. Now just imagine being there for ETERNITY. Sound like fun? Didn't think so.

At any rate, that was why I was confused about the whole Gabby situation. I mean, I knew that the whole "patch on my arm" thing was bullshit. I knew that I felt better the instant she touched me, but after that I was just baffled. Was it because Gabby possessed some weird mojo that could make vertigo disappear? Or was it that I've been here so long that I was actually craving human contact? And why had she touched me? Did she know that she would heal me? Or was it more of that "trying to make me more comfortable" thing that she had going on. And, while I'm asking myself a bunch of mind-fuck questions, how did she get away with that? I mean, all I did was help a guy get back online and BOOM... don't let the door hit you in the ass on the way out! She made coffee for fuck's sake! GOOD coffee at that!

So my mind is a jumble, but I'm still feeling good overall when I get to the office at the end of the hall. The door is now slightly ajar, so after a moment of consternation, wondering if I should knock or just walk in, I hear that lovely voice come from inside. "Do come in Louise, I think we've both been put on hold long enough."

When I walked through the door I had about 3 seconds to take in my surroundings. If I had known that I only had 3 seconds I would've paid more attention more quickly. However, I didn't. So, all I got was the temperature in this man's office was SUBLIME. It wasn't cool, but it wasn't hot either. It felt like early summer after a drenching rain. It felt...well, *fresh*. Where exactly in the LITERAL Hell am I? How is this happening? Oh and the chairs, have I mentioned the chairs yet?? None of these chairs look broken, or wobbly, or look like they could moonlight as torture devices. In other words, they don't look like any chair I've ever seen in Hell! They looked comfy, and soft, and I really want to sit in them.

I also notice one of those nameplates that people always have on their desks. Why do people have those things? Pure vanity — or maybe they occasionally forget who they are? Then of course I realized, I didn't know this guy's name, so perhaps they do have a use. I glanced at it, registering the name MR. DEEDY just as Mr. Deedy himself unleashed like a tornado.

"Hello Louise May Patterson!" It was almost sing-song. He was so enthused. "Born, according to your resume, on April 6, Year of Our Lord, as they say, 1957 and expired on October 3, 2000. You've been wallowing in the depths ever since. You were employed in life as...." He stops to page through a short document on very nice parchment that has my name typed across the top... "well, guess not. And employed in Hell at the infamous IP&FW where you were recently terminated due to — ah, due to actually helping someone." He begins to laugh. "Silly girl. They HATE that at IP&FW. Do have a seat. Let's chat a while."

I sink into one of the chairs and immediately fall in love —with a chair. I'm never getting up. This chair is more comfortable than my bed.

Now, despite the fact that he did not take a break, or even a breath here,

I'm taking a break just to make my head stop spinning. Mr. Deedy is not like anyone I've ever met or seen. EVER. First of all, he's REALLY tall. Like basketball player tall. You know in those old cowboy movies when the gunslinger would come to town and the saloon girl would sidle up to him and say in a seductive voice "My goodness, ain't you a tall drink of water!" Well, that gunslinger would have to stand on a stool to look Mr. Deedy in the eye. And thin. To call him wiry would be insulting to wires. Heroin addicts probably feel fat around him. My friend Bonnie from high school had an eating disorder and used to pass out in the middle of a sentence, and she wasn't as thin as him.

He's odd to be sure. When he first approached me I held out my hand to shake his, like every job interview I've ever seen on TV or in a movie, and since that is my only frame of reference I expected him to grab my hand and say "Firm handshake, good sign!" or something. But instead, he kept right on talking and looked down at my hand then looked at me and shook his head '*no*' while he continued his non-stop diatribe. Who does that? Maybe he's OCD or a germaphobe, but who would be afraid of germs after they're dead? I wonder if he's afraid to touch Gabby. He probably should touch her, and she'd get rid of whatever freaky thing he has that makes him leave a girl hangin' with her hand stuck out like a panhandler. Or perhaps whatever country he's from doesn't do the handshake thing. Maybe they kiss each other's cheeks or whatever. I honestly do not know about stuff like that, because European television and movies are boring and stuffy, and no one exotic ever comes to the town that I lived in when I was alive. By exotic I mean anyone who's from anywhere other than the tri-county area, let alone from another country.

He's not particularly good-looking. He looks almost cartoonish... sharp features, pointed and very prominent nose, teeth that don't sit right in his mouth so his tongue seems to be moving around in there like it's pushing them to the side when he speaks, big eyes like a porcelain figurine, wild hair. Which, by the way, appears to be created by product. I giggle at the thought of Mr. Deedy walking into one of the chain stores and asking the clerk with 17 layers of make-up on her face where he can find hair gel. He carries himself like a little boy pretending to be a man, with his chest stuck out and never knowing quite what to do with all those limbs. All of that combined with his height and lack of girth and Deedy makes one Hell of an impression.

Nevertheless, when he laughs, his whole face comes along for the ride and his eyes get a little sparkly. And you can tell just by looking at him that he's kind. Not necessarily sweet, nor gentle, but always kind. He instantly makes you wonder if he's an actual resident here, or maybe he's like a social worker from Heaven, who commutes down here to help out poor schlubs like me.

That would explain a lot, like the comfy chairs and the temperature in his office. It would also explain what he's wearing. Unlike the rest of us who find a new nightmare in our closet each day, this man is dressed to the nines. A beautiful suit that looks like it was tailored specifically to him is draping across his long, lean body in absolute perfection — the exact brown of his eyes, which is both a thing of beauty and a little disquieting.

The suit looks expensive too, while everything down here is cheap and badly-made. If Giorgio Armani was dead (and who knows? he might be by now) I'd be pretty sure he'd made that suit.

"Louise, still with me?" he looked at me expectantly.

"Of course!" Shit, I lost almost half of what he was saying. And that's a bunch, considering how he's machine-gunning words towards me at the speed of light. "I was just a bit distracted, admiring your suit. I mean pardon my French, but that is fucking beautiful. Where did it come from?"

"I was saying that according to this" he looks down again at the resume that I have NO IDEA how he obtained, "that since you found our notice you've been plagued with fake memories, emotional reactions well beyond anything you've experienced here, and dreams, none of which you remember right? Oh, and that will be 25 cents." He reaches under the desk and pulls out a jar with the words "CURSE JAR" printed on it. He's very nonchalant, never taking his eyes off the document.

"Huh?" I'm now confused on several levels. What resume, especially one that I didn't write or submit, talks about dreams? Granted, I've never even seen a real live resume, let alone created one, but I'm pretty sure that they stick to skill sets and former jobs, not private personal fantasies or dreams! Especially dreams that I didn't know I was having, since according to the aforementioned bizarre resume I can't remember them. And the curse jar must be a joke, right? Should I laugh, or just ignore it?

Deedy turns and faces me. "I can't possibly 'pardon your French' as you've asked me to unless you put a quarter in this jar. And by the way, that word is in no way, shape, or form French. It's Middle English in origin, originally '*fucken*' which means to strike, move quickly, or penetrate. How it became the most popular verb, adjective, noun, AND insult in the English language is beyond me. However, it'll cost you a quarter." He seems bemused, but he's still holding out the jar. He's expecting me to put 25 cents in there.

"Are you serious? Or are you fucking with me?" I ask, truly bewildered.

"See? Since you've entered my office you used it as a complimentary adjective and a derogatory verb, neither of which would indicate striking, moving fast, or penetrating. There are now 1,009,614 words in your native tongue. Why do you make that word work so hard? Nor is it, for your information and edification, normal conversation fodder at a job interview. And now, it's 50 cents."

Okay, so now I'm vacillating between feeling bad, because he's right... It's awful to walk into a stranger's office trying to pretend to be any kind of professional and start talking like a sailor on leave... But there's also the principal of the thing, which is that a curse jar is stupid and I'm not giving him 50 cents. So, I react the way I always react when I'm not sure if I'm right but I'm bound and determined to convince someone else that I am. In other words I *over-react*.

"Mr. Deedy, I apologize for coming here and offending you. As you can tell by my apparent resume, that is and will be forever a mystery to me, I am not well-educated or well-versed in these kinds of proceedings. Obviously I am highly unqualified for whatever it is I'm here to interview for, and so I'll go. I promise to put the job notice back where I found it and I can only hope that this simple act will encourage you to take out that weird phone that showed up in my apartment and also forgive my overwhelming debt! Having said all that, I just want you to know that I do not appreciate your condescending manner of pointing out my uneducated speech or your feeble attempts at embarrassing me or making me feel like a giant shitbird. I cannot abide that kind of treatment. Good day, Mr. Deedy!" I say all this with an increasing frenzy so that by the time I'm done I've risen from my seat and I'm practically in tears. Oscar goes to... me.

Mr. Deedy looks at me with a half-smile and one eyebrow raised up higher than the other. It's not threatening, or apologetic, or even amused. It's just a simple look, yet I feel like I've been struck, hit with some invisible force that takes my breath away. Not to mention it's like he's gazing into my soul with those penetrating brown eyes and scanning all my bullshit in a millisecond. He glances at the chair and then back to me, and as I sink into it I reach into my pocket and pull out 75 cents and drop it into the jar.

He then returns to the resume and continues as though nothing has happened. "So, I'd like you to tell me exactly what you remember about the years approaching your demise. I assume your memory is somewhat blotchy, correct? And I'll also need to know precisely what a shitbird is, and why, not to mention where, they seemingly carry change?"

Yep, I think to myself, I have just been *'fuckened'*.

Deedy was equivalent to my afterlife as meeting Linda in life. Not that we milk-shaked all over each other, but that his impact was instant and measurable. He had put me in my place, but also at ease simultaneously. He is not like any man I've ever remembered meeting. To my amazement (since I only heard of these men in fairy stories) he's no bull-shitter and won't try to con me. He can be frustrating, sometimes a little condescending, and seems to be amused by me but he's never even tried to use manipulation, or mind-games, or his own ego against me. I would not call him nice, or sweet, or polite; Yet he made me feel comfortable, even as he was chastising me for my potty mouth. I would say it's like meeting a member of your own family, yet it is different even from that. It's not like your dad, who loves you unconditionally but whose approval you are constantly trying to get anyway... with Deedy, it's never about approval or doing the right thing.. it's more like fulfilling some great potential that only he can see. Which is why when the interview took a left turn I wasn't sure where I was headed, to a temp job or back to the street.

"Why do you want to know about the years before I died?" I asked, once I recovered from the whole curse jar experience.

"Because we here at Second Chance Temp Agency believe that we cannot find you a perfect placement if we don't know anything about the person being placed." said Deedy in his best infomercial sales pitch voice. "No really" he continued, more sincerely. "This isn't just an opportunity for you to work, Louise. It's... well, it's just an *opportunity*. Take advantage of it, and enjoy the company for a little while. Shall I have Gabby bring us some more coffee?"

To be quite honest, I liked the idea of keeping company with Mr. Deedy in his lovely office that felt like a vacation from my usual Hellish existence, and I loved the idea of more of Gabby's wonderful coffee, so I sat back and started to talk.

"Don't you people prefer tea?" I asked teasingly. "Which people would that be?" he asked me with the same ribbing tone, almost with an excitement of the chance to see what I would say. Great, I'm now being tested on where he's from.

"English people... or maybe Irish people?" I said, then quickly "or Scottish?"

He laughed. "Welsh people, darling girl." Then he said the strangest thing... he didn't talk about where he was born or about his family or his life. He simply said "I've always had an affinity for the Welsh. You know in Wales the daffodil is considered a work of art, and sheep outnumber people 4 to 1!" he looks at me with expectation, like I should "ooooo" and "ahhhh" over that fact.

"Sounds boring." I replied. "Almost as boring as where I grew up."

Deedy then nestled in his seat and rested his chin on his hands, another boyish move from a seemingly grown man. And said, "Time to tell me all about it."

Having to talk out loud about my life and subsequent death was surreal. I've never told my story to anyone, and after all this time (however much time it has been) I can't really remember which parts actually happened and which parts are little fantasies I've made up since being here. I talked about my lifestyle, who I was, who I imagined myself to be, but when Deedy started asking me specifically about my late 30's and early 40's I couldn't unlock anything specific. I tried to fill in the gaps with stuff that sounded like it could be true, but he knew when I was making it up as I went along and he would stop me and smile and say "Louise, for now you can say 'I can't remember'. I'd prefer that to your version of a horrifying bedtime story." Everyone's a critic.

So, I told him about my mom and dad and Linda. I told him about Hank and how the day before Linda's wedding I had a huge bachelorette party and got totally wasted and begged her not to marry him. I told him about my cancer, and about how I remember lying in bed with people around me, but I can't imagine who all those people would be, and I told him about my Mom talking but I don't remember what she said, and then I told him about waking up under the overpass and realizing I was damned for eternity and how that's been working out for me. I rambled on and on and Deedy actually listened to every single word. He laughed when I tried to be funny, he cooed when I tried to be wistful, and when I tried to invoke emotion by talking about my regrets and fears he looks at me like I'm full of shit.

"What? I'm not allowed be contrite because I ended up in Hell?" I say after one of those 'oh please' looks from Deedy. "Of course you can. But here's what I wonder... "

I waited. For a while. Then I finally explode with exasperation. "Wonder about???"

He looked at me, looked into me. His eyes locked on mine and for a minute I actually got goosebumps. There was a fire in his stare, like his eyes were made of the same stuff as Hell itself. It was like he was a peeping Tom but instead of looking at my body through a window, he was looking at my soul, which actually felt more intimate than if I were standing in front of him naked. Then suddenly it was over, and Deedy was back to being the little boy stuck inside a grown man's body. His face and eyes filled with laughter and kindness once again.

"I wonder how you feel about garbage?" He said suddenly.

"Garbage? I can honestly say that I've never spent a single moment of my life or afterlife contemplating it in any way." I say with a hint of disgust.

"Well, my darling girl, that is about to change!" said Deedy with the enthusiasm of a game show telling me I'd just won a million dollars. But instead of a million dollars, he handed me a small yellow slip of paper with an address on it.

"What is this? A piece of trash I'm supposed to think about?" I said.

Deedy laughed out loud. "Nope. This is your first temp job. You Louise May Patterson are now in the waste management industry!"

"A Garbage Man?" I say weakly, my stomach already starting to turn.

Okay, so I think that I accidentally lied to Deedy. I have actually thought about garbage. Well, more specifically, I've thought about garbage collection. There was a brief affair once with a guy who owned a trash collection company — married of course. He found himself out and about each Wednesday morning trucking around suburbia, a landscape consistently cluttered by both trash cans and bored housewives. It didn't take long to find his true calling, which was collecting conquests as well as rubbish. The coffee klatches in town were full of twittering middle-aged women who spoke in whispers of Don "the trash man" and his sexual repertoire. Eventually the rumors trickled down into my crowd. So, as a public service of course, I decided to find out what could be proven or denied.

To that purely altruistic end, I stood outside one Wednesday morning and watched as his truck hopscotched its way down my street picking up cans from either side with a lumbering zig-zag that just screams

GARBAGE TRUCK. Don "the trash man" was a very handsome African-American man (not Denzel good-looking, but damn close for this town) with a body built by manual labor. In the morning sun he looked like he had been chiseled out of ebony. What can I say? I was ready to approach this pursuit of truth with gusto. Occasionally he'd stop and talk to someone, usually female. She'd have a cold drink or a plate of some baked good to offer him and they seemed to be having harmless conversation, about the weather or a local sports event. When in reality they were probably planning an encounter for later in the day. That guy's appointment book must have looked like a doctor's office diary. He must have ordered Viagra by the case. When he finally got to my house, I was acting as disinterested in him or his truck as I could muster, instead pretending to be studying something terribly important in the yard — as if there was anything in my front yard to hold my interest at that hour of the morning aside from the prospect of getting laid by a semi-pro.

"You up early or just going to bed?" he said to me that first morning — just kind of jumped right in, so to speak.

I answered him with the same flirty tone of voice. "Figured I'd come see what all the fuss is about. You know, the whole 'early bird' propaganda that you hear all the time."

"So you're birdwatching?" he said with a sly smile.

"No... I'm out here hunting for a worm." I returned. (Yes, the double-entrendres were flying like bullets in a Dirty Harry movie.)

He finished with the can in front of my house and had just set it down, empty. So I fired off a question. "So what happens if you have to pee while you are on your route? Are you allowed to knock on someone's door and ask to use their powder room?"

Now, believe it or not, I have used the "what if you have to pee" question as a pick-up line on many occasions. All with great success. Whether it's a paraplegic, or the guy standing in front of the seafood restaurant in a lobster suit, or the garbage man... the response is always the same.

"Wow," said Don, laughing. "You are the first person to ever ask me that question!" Then he looked at me with new eyes, as if to say 'this one's got moxy!'

It was as if I'd written the script and he was right on cue.

Then he started to tell me about various public restrooms or porta-pottys on his route and how one learns how to time where and when they stop for coffee in coordination with how far one is from the nearest public facility. Then he said the most horrifying thing I've ever heard in my life. "But I always keep a mayonnaise jar under the front seat in case my calculations are off."

Now I know that you want to hear now is how I lured him into my house, which was consequently empty due to the fact that my mother had gone to the nearest city with my aunt on a shopping trip and my dad was of course, at work. And you'll also be wanting to hear about all the nasty things he did to me on my mom's kitchen counters. And how she never knew it because if she had, she would have set fire to them or possibly ripped them up with her bare hands before ever preparing food on them again. And how when you mix someone as practiced and proficient as Don the trash man and someone as committed to the craft of freakdom as me, you are able for a few brief moments, over a few brief encounters, to raise the mere sport fuck to a fiery level of passion that can only be described as an art form.

But unfortunately, I cannot tell you about that. Because now all I can think about is that mayonnaise jar.

As I'm walking back from the interview (I had foregone the idea of finding the special tagged cabbie to take me home), that is the one distracting thought that keeps ricocheting around inside my brain. I'm in Hell, and I've just secured a job that requires a mayonnaise jar under the best of circumstances... which would be in the land of the living... and I'm stuck in 'the-worst-case-scenario' world.

As I reach my apartment I'm totally spent. What a crazy day. I am emotionally, mentally, and physically exhausted. Today I discovered a phone where before there was none. I met a telepath — pretty sure the first one ever in my experience. I went higher into the abyss we call a sky down here than ever before. I had the best cup of coffee in Hell, I'm almost certain. I sat in pure comfort for a little while, and talked to another person about something more substantial than how hot it is, or what I wanted to eat or just to say "Fuck you!" for the first time since arriving here. And that other person happens to be Deedy, the most remarkable being I've ever met in life or the afterlife. I survived my first ever job interview, and even came out employed, something I probably could be quite proud of if I had the energy.

Yet, as I stumble up to my tiny apartment and collapse on the bed, I kick off my mary janes and allow myself to drift off with one singular thought...

You just know I'm going to have to pee in a jar tomorrow.

7

Epic dreaming. When I was alive I used to love those few and far-between nights when my brain would decide that it was going to entertain me — creating in my subconscious this delicious story that played out like a film with grand cinematography and everything. Epic dreams are always fictional, but with great metaphorical value. And they usually star me and my friends doing amazing things, like flying through jungles (sans aircraft since we can actually fly!!) or swashbuckling on a pirate ship, or hanging out at some fancy nightclub with our favorite pop stars. And the next day, while it was still fresh in my memory I'd call up Linda or some other friend who had made an appearance in the night before show and tell them every detail of the dream. And then we would start analyzing what the dream meant.

"Maybe flying means letting go of something, or someone...or maybe it just means getting high!"

"I read in a book once that swords and knives in dreams mean penises."

"But I got to slow dance with Liam while you were singing the Titanic theme on stage!"

"Wait, so if I stabbed you with a sword, does that mean that I wish I had a penis??"

It would go on and on and by the time it was all said and done, the dream was worth a few laughs, an argument or two, and the occasional "Do you think I'm actually gay?" heart-to-heart conversation.

Epic dreams stay with you, sometimes for days, always replaying in the back of your mind. That's what makes epic dreaming so wonderful — unless of course, you are in Hell. which, as I've made it abundantly clear, I am.

Down here epic dreams are never fictional, but they are crystal clear and stick with you like glue. They are vivid memories, but not ones that I yearn to see again. They are the acts and deeds that brought me here in the first place. You know how people say when you die your life "flashes before your eyes"? I wish that were true. Because a flash of what I've done would be hard to witness, to be sure, but it would be over quickly and then I could move onto the next adventure. But to have to relive those moments, in great detail, over and over for eternity — that is the greatest punishment the devil or whoever is responsible for this wretched place could inflict upon me or any of us. When we first met I said that dreams are the one thing Hell can't take away, but that is not the whole story. Hell can also give nightmares, and the worst part about it is, these nightmares have already come true. My nightmares are my past, and the burden I carry with me down here, getting heavier with them every day, week, month and year that I'm forced to confront them.

So when I sit up in bed this morning I know why my face is drenched with tears. I don't even hit the snooze button today, because today I'd rather be anywhere than in bed where I've just relived one of the darkest days of my life. That was the day before Linda got married.

Now let me explain. It's not like I just decided to pop a nutty at Linda's big night out with no warning or provocation. There was a significant pattern that led up to my behavior long before the fateful bachelorette party. I had witnessed the proverbial writing on the wall well in advance of that night. From the first moment that she burst into my room at Mom and Dad's and showed me the ring and asked me to be her maid of honor (and yes, I know how ridiculous that sounds, but who else would she ask?) I was in full-blown panic at the prospect of what was about to happen.

And, in Hank's defense, it wasn't just the fact that she was marrying him, or the fact that she was marrying at all. It was all about to change. Linda was leaving me behind so that she could go play grown-up with a job and a car and a husband... and eventually she'd probably have babies and carpools and parent-teacher conferences. Linda was meant for so much more than bake sales and soccer practice. She was supposed to transcend with me to a higher purpose. To be forever young — a child of the universe that floats and coaxes whatever she needs and leaves it all to luck and chance and chaos, if for no other reason than just to see what would happen. That is what true intelligence and beauty and loving life is about. It's about not falling into any of the traps that society sets for us to try and make us be what they are. It's about seeking adventure and wringing every bit of fun you can get out of living. Leave the breeding for the mainstream. We are better than those folks, and why couldn't Linda see that?

That was the exact bullshit I said to my best friend on the eve of her wedding. Only I was so drunk it came out as one giant, slurry, run-on sentence with the occasional "fuck me, I lost my train of thought" or "hey cutie, what are you doing later?" or "Who do you have to blow to get a shot of tequila around here?" thrown in for good measure. Oh, and did I mention that I said all of that in the form of a toast, in front of all her friends — and family?

And that includes her mom and 83 year-old grandmother.

I finished my diatribe with this pearl of wisdom:

"Would you like to know the secret of the universe, kids? Cuz I've got it right here. Men always want what they can't have, and never want what they've got. And women always want what they used to have and they will settle for anything or anyone that gives them the illusion that they can have it back. And there will be moments, and this might actually be one for our Linda, when you can actually sit back and say that you are content, almost happy with your life, with yourself and the one standing next to you... and you should embrace those moments, because they will all go away— quickly."

And in my nightmare, as in life, I sat down to an awkward silence that would have been quite embarrassing if I weren't so clueless or wasted. Everyone was squirming in their seats or looking at me like I'd just reached up into my own nose and pulled out a giant slug and set it free on their fucking table. Finally, after what seemed like hours, Linda got up and raised her glass and said:

"Lou, you aren't exactly being fair. Maybe I've hijacked a seat on this ride long enough. Because after all, let's face it, I've never really been as intelligent or beautiful or charming as you... have I?"

Everyone in the room burst out laughing. They all walked up to Linda and patted her on the back and said how great a retort that was, and how she was showing so much class and how perhaps she should consider her friendship with me like having a Barbie or Mr. Potato Head, something you leave behind with nostalgia and good memories but you can't muster up the patience to play with anymore.

But here's the part that makes me feel like I deserve Hell more than you know. Amidst the laughter and congratulatory "zinger" comments, and the alcohol fog that I was in, Linda and I locked gazes and I knew, at that moment, I knew that she *meant* what she said. And it broke my heart to know. It broke my heart that she, the most wonderful thing that had come into my life, could still think I was smart and funny and beautiful even as I was humiliating her and myself at a party where she was supposed to be the center of attention. I was always a spotlight whore, and considered bad attention better than no attention. However, tonight was supposed to be Linda's and I had pissed all over her parade. Here we were, on the night before the most important day of her life, and her best friend/maid of honor (stop rolling your eyes every time I say that) is not being supportive or excited for her or making sure she's making memories to enjoy in her old age. No, instead I acted like an ass, and in the process somehow maybe reminded her that I could have actually been right. Perhaps Linda was choosing to settle, and most probably she was happy, a lot of the time, being trapped for a change. It had to be refreshing to not have to be "on" all the time, and to not have to be second fiddle to her psychotic best friend. However, her friend's and family's reaction to my inspired (yet, granted, grossly inappropriate) toast was just a reminder that she was once a person who could say and do anything she wanted or thought without remorse or fear.

Still, all those revelations aside, she was really pissed at me. Later, after everyone had begged off and gone home, she and I sat at the bar drinking after hours with the bartender who threw caution and possibly his ABC license to the wind and kept on serving us.

"You know, I understand why you are such a huge bitch. I just don't understand why you pick these times to display it." she said with a twinge of resignation in her voice.

"Sorry babe." I said, and I meant it. "I just panicked. I'm feeling abandoned so I lashed out. What's that saying about you only hurt the ones you love?"

"I think it's a song, actually. And it doesn't matter. What matters is that we are always going to be friends. You are always going to need me, to call at 2 a.m. for a ride or to pick apart a dream or a new guy. And I am still going to sit by the phone and wait for that call, and be just a little jealous of you as I've always been. But my life is going to look different now. People grow up, Lou. Even you may have to face it one day. Just because we allow ourselves to change doesn't mean that we failed at what we were doing before, it just means that we're allowing it to turn into something else."

"Letting the past become the future." I say, trying to sound profound.

"THERE'S the secret to the universe, kid!" Linda said laughing.

"Yeah, well let's not forget that Ms. Margarita has some serious culpability for that little speech!" I responded, as I waved to the bartender for another round.

"Maybe she can talk my Mother off the ledge so that she won't tackle you to keep you out of the church tomorrow." said Linda.

"So you are really going through with it?" I said, with a just a bit of sadness.

"Yup."

"Then I, your maid of dishonor, will be there with bells on. And no one, not even your scary mother will be able to stop me!" I said as I lifted my glass.

That is where I woke up this morning, disappointed at myself all over again. Not to mention feeling just a teensy bit sorry for myself that I was able to prove Linda wrong and never actually grow up or old. That, along with feeling the accompanying exhaustion that comes from a night of epic nightmares, forces my head down on the heated window pane as I lift my face (with eyes closed to prevent the blinding effects) to the sky and say "Sorry Linda, Hope today you are happier than you were yesterday, and I hope all your tomorrows are wonderful."

I drag myself out of bed and take a peek inside my closet. It takes a moment for my brain to register why there is an orange jumpsuit hanging in there with my name over the left breast pocket. Oh yeah, Today is my first day at work.

8

I pause briefly around the coffee shop area thinking I might get a cup before work, but then the mayonnaise jar thought occurs to me, so I skip it. I'm counting on dehydration to get me through this experience.
I'm also kind of enjoying my jaunt to employment today. Because while on earth wearing an orange jumpsuit would be a veritable testimony to the bad choices you had made so far in your life, in Hell it's obviously clear that poor judgement was pretty much a ruling factor during your time as a breather. Paying for it now day after day at the devil's leisure would, you'd think, build up a sense of camaraderie down here. But, since most of us showed no real humanity when we were actually human, I guess that would be too much to ask for in the land of the damned.

So down here the rule is "he who doesn't look as uncomfortable as me should be hated, sneered at, and glared down on the street". And if you are one of the ones who is wearing something that looks like it may not be pinching you in your naughty bits or riding up the naughtier ones, you feel free to gloat about it.

And, while orange has never been a good color for me, and it denotes the fact that I'm a garbage man, it's not exactly an uncomfortable outfit. So, I'm doing my share of gloating this morning. I even smile and wave at the folks that I pass on the street, who naturally shoot invisible daggers into my midriff with their evil stares.

Besides the jumpsuit, I'm thinking that this could be a whole new start for me down here — making the best of a shitty situation, as it were. Well, in reality, the shittiest situation ever. But still, a new start with a new job, with clothes that can be mildly tolerated if not necessarily catwalk material. And I get to be out and about, and I get a change of scenery, always miserable, but changing — right?

So, feeling as optimistic as one could under my circumstances, I round the corner to the trash collection company. TCC for short. The smell hits me before I even get within eyesight of the place, and all my optimism is drowned in an ocean of noxious fumes. It's a clinging, sticky kind of stink — the kind you know is going to take refuge inside your nose and start screaming 'Sancuary!' Sort of like Quasimodo every time you attempt to sniff or blow it out. It's the kind of smell that is usually hard-wired into your gag reflex, but of course down here there really isn't a clear path from your digestive tract to the street, what with being a construct and all, so I get kind of green around the gills but never actually boot.

I stumble into the building marked with the Trash Collection Company logo hoping for some relief. But I just find that in an enclosed space, even the enormous office complex that is TCC, the stench is more concentrated. I don't know whether to breathe from my mouth, and risk somehow tasting this Hellish smell, or just say 'fuck it' and stop breathing altogether. I mean, what's the worst that could happen? Breathing has got to be optional in the afterlife right? So I give it a try and actually hold my breath. When I start to feel lightheaded and lose all peripheral vision I surrender and take a deep breath, followed by a strange choking noise from the fact that my throat is actually closing to keep the odor out. Damn all of us and our illusion of life!

I stumble over to the reception desk and can barely speak. The girl behind the desk should be named Anti-Gabby, since she's the diametric opposite of Gabby in Deedy's office. Instead of floating around passing out coffee and making a girl feel better with a single touch, this girl is rooted to a chair, filing nails that are now sharpened points at the end of her fingers. She's chomping on gum and looks at me with an expression that is the perfect blend of boredom, torment, and disgust. How awful it must be for her to work in this malodorous environment. I flashback on a movie I saw once where the characters were exiled to a bog of stench, and the guard there had no idea how bad it was, since he'd been there so long. It was like his nostrils had burned away the smell. Even though the movie was a fantasy, and it didn't take place on earth, it obviously also didn't take place in Hell. I don't think here anyone gets used to anything. That's part of the whole "damnation" thing, right? I mean, how many people do you know right now who are stuck in a life, or a marriage, or a place, or just a state of being that makes you think 'If that were me, I'd have already run a hot bath and opened up a packet of razor blades.' Yet, they go on... because it is the life they've gotten used to, and they can't imagine anything better. How would it be if in Hell we all became complacent or even *content*. That would hardly be a punishment. And we are here to be punished, to be sure. For time endless.

Anyway, working here has done nothing for Anti-Gabby's disposition, which could not have been great in the first place, being as she was sentenced to the aforementioned eternal damnation. And she can't have been pleased when she got into her closet this morning, considering her pants suit is made of a quite porous muslin dyed a pukey green color and highlighted with dark brown spots that could have been put there by a designer but looks more like baby diarrhea. I stop for a moment to wonder if every day she has a particularly odor-absorbent outfit waiting for her or if she's being particularly punished today. I wonder if I asked if she would answer. Then, by looking again at the scowl with which she greeted me, and still holds on me like a gun during a mugging, I quickly figure that the answer would be 'no.' She's probably not exactly the forthcoming type. Speaking of, I also stop to notice that in front of her is an old-fashioned switchboard with lights and small buzzers going off, apparently to deaf ears. She's not even looked at it, let alone answer a single call.

There were a couple of folks at IP&FW who used to just put people on hold and never go back to them. They were usually picked to be employees of the month. If I were feeling more gracious I'd tell her to go down and there and put in an application, but well...no, this is not a place where I want to make new friends, and it's not exactly like she's been the most gracious hostess as of yet. So instead I clear my throat as best as I can and croak out "Hello. My name is..."

"Louise Patterson!" a booming male voice from behind me finishes my sentence. I turn around and find a huge man dressed in a very similar to mine jumpsuit (except that his is filthy) and the grubbiest beard I've ever laid eyes on. Why would he, if it's true that we're all just figments of our own imagination, bring that fetid beard to Hell with him? And when I say he's huge I don't mean tall and lean like Deedy or muscular like Don the trash man — I mean fat —terribly fat. His enormous belly, although confined by the jumpsuit, is still able to hang over to touch his knees. That, and the beard and he looks like a demented Santa Claus. Suddenly, I'm scared to respond to my own name.

"O.K.?" I finally say, strangely posing it as a question.

"You're back here in the truck bay." he motions for me to follow him.

Damn. For a minute I was thinking 'Yeah, they have office workers at trash companies too! Maybe I'll be sitting behind a desk filing my nails all day." But no, not me — I'm on a truck. Do you think they have partners? Will I have to hang with someone else all day? Oh shit! Please don't let it be scary Santa! And what if there's not a partner? Do I even know how to drive a truck? I'm pretty sure I never drove anything bigger than a Camry in real life. Crap. Where did he go?

I was so lost in that little thought bubble that I forgot to pay attention to the behemoth of a man in front of me and he somehow got away. Fuck me. Now what do I do? I'm standing at a hallway and looking down both corridors for the man. Apparently he's more spry than his formidable frame would allow you to think he was, because he's gone. A younger man with a clipboard walks by. I stop him to ask him where the truck bay is when I realize, *I know that face...* I recognize the smirk it's wearing! "Will?" I ask incredulously. "What are you doing here?" It took a minute because he wasn't wearing the organ-grinder suit that he had at the agency, but it was Will alright!

"Hmmmmm...." he says, as if giving himself time to think of an excuse. "Working?"

"Were you sent to spy on me?" I don't know whether to be pissed off or flattered. Why would Deedy or the agency send someone out to watch me? Do they think I'm a huge fucktard or are they making sure I'm okay? Will seems taken aback by my question, like he wasn't expecting me to come right out and ask.

"Not exactly spying," he offered. "Just here to make sure all is well."

He said it with such a reassuring tone that it made me feel like I was in kindergarten again and had spotted my Mom hiding behind a tree on the playground at recess — watching over me, making sure I was okay.

"Alright then. Can you get me to the truck bay?" I ask.

"Follow me." he says as he takes my arm and we walk down the corridor.

"Truck Bay." Will announced like he was still on the elevator announcing what floor we were on. "And by the way Louise, do you realize that you are 20 minutes early?"

Shit! Being punctual may be the way to go in the land of the living, but in Hell it is right up there with being helpful. I should have been at least a little late. Maybe had Will take me all around the stinkified building before reporting for duty. But now I'm here and Bad Santa is looking me over like I'm a Christmas cookie. Ugh. I walked up to him and immediately started in with my excuse-making. "Sorry I'm early, but the walk wasn't as long as I thought," when he started to laugh.

"Not to worry cupcake, the only thing worse than hearing a garbage truck coming down your street first thing in the morning, is hearing a garbage truck coming down your street a half an hour EARLY." Then he patted me on the bottom and took me to see my newest and shiniest nightmare yet.

I am now sitting in the biggest truck I've ever experienced. You wouldn't believe it, but the stench is actually diminished inside the cab of the truck. It is still there, and it is still really bad. It's also even more apparent because it's mixed with the revolting "gas-station-restroom-that-has-just-been-cleaned" smell of pine, coming from a small green cardboard tree hanging off the rear-view mirror. But I'm not on the verge of hurling anymore. Well, let me clarify. I don't feel like I'm going to hurl from stinkiness anymore. Now I'm on the verge of a panic attack because they expect me to drive this truck— all by myself! Bad Santa just tossed me the keys and said "Map's on the dash." Not before he tried to grab my ass again, but this time I shot him a look that said 'I'm not the run-to-HR-to-file-a-formal-complaint kind of a gal. I'm the girl that will find something sharp and do a dichotomy on you faster than you can blink.' And while I'm sure that poor, old, scary Santa hasn't been face-to-face with his Johnson in quite a few years (before and after death), he seemed committed to keeping it, because his hand was in his pocket for the rest of our meeting.

And so here I am — not even sure where or how to start the ignition on this thing. I probably shouldn't have scared him that badly. He may have given me a few pointers before he scurried off back in the direction of the truck bay. Back to the truck, I'm kind of in awe of how everything in here seems bigger than it should be. I bet I look tiny in here. That's a fact I would have liked to have had when I was alive. No need to diet, girls! Just hang out inside of really big things and you'll look small! The steering wheel is actually bigger around than my arm span. That should make cornering a breeze, right?

Also, there are more pedals on the floor than I have feet, so what the fuck??

What doesn't escape me is that this giant machine, this mechanical monstrosity, has a sole purpose — to move garbage from one place to another. Isn't that remarkable? You have it on your world as well —

great, huge heaps of unwanted waste piling up, spreading out and filling your world with the same stench and burning piles that are now part of my eternal life. I was never a tree hugger in life, and I wouldn't consider myself an activist in any way — even now. But I have to admit that I just hate to think that the world above is slowly turning itself into another version of Hell. And for what? For convenience? Out of laziness? Out of sheer disrespect for what you've got? Well, just wait. Because some of you are bound to end up here, and you'll see what your children and grandchildren have to look forward to once you've piled up enough trash and polluted your air and water to the point where Eternal Hell will seem like a vacation to Club Med.

Okay, enough with the soapbox. I have to drive. And I think I'm going to need my whole brain to concentrate on this particular task. I look around the cab and find an old manual. Bunches of pages are missing, and I assume they are very important pages (because why else would they be missing?) I do find instructions on how to start the damn thing. Get this, there's a key, and a button, and a gear shift in the floor that all have to be put or pushed or turned the right way in the correct order just to start the motor! Who comes up with this? After six or seven tries I finally get it started and running. Now I have to actually get it moving. The pedal that I assume is the "go" pedal, since it's on the far right, is surprisingly touchy. The second my toes just brush up against it I'm jerking forward. Maybe it drives just like a car, only bigger. That thought, along with the accelerator propels me forward until I get out of the garage and it's time to turn onto the street. This giant mountain of a truck turned against me and started to work in opposition. 'Okay' I think to myself, 'So it's going to be a fight!' I use all of my strength to keep the wheels turning in the right direction. The maps on the dash slide off and onto the floor, but if I know Hell like I think I do, they are probably useless anyway, so I just start looking for cans on the street. When I see one up ahead I start to brake.

Note to self: braking in a big ass truck is totally different than braking in a compact car. DUH.

I hit the brake and it's like the pedal is not attached to an actual mechanism that goes to the wheels and forces them to stop. It's more like the brake pedal is the nerd who got invited accidentally to a big wheel frat party and finds itself whispering a suggestion to one of the wheels, who turns and glares at the brake like he's the biggest moron at the party, but then eventually sees the error of his ways and reconsiders. However, in a feeble attempt to preserve what little pride the wheel has left, it doesn't just stop immediately, it has to do it at its own pace — so that later, when it gets ribbed by the other wheels it can say it was its own decision to stop, and had virtually nothing to do with anything the brake said to it at any time.

Yes, for you wondering, I had time to come up with that ridiculous metaphor while waiting for the fucking truck to come to halt.

Just as I come to a stop, my heart follows the truck and freezes like ice when I suddenly see a small blonde head running in front of the garbage truck. I burst out of the cab and start to walk around the truck so that I can see the apparent child. Even though I know that death has already happened to everyone here, I realize that I'm not quite breathing right now. I assume there are two reasons.

One, you don't get to see many kids down here. There are kids, but they weren't children in life. Well, they started out as children — as we all did — but some folks are not given the option to come here as they were when they passed. Some people are just too bad for Hell even. They would get down here and just see a reflection of the world they left behind. They would see it as a playground. So, when they emerge from the dark they find themselves literally playground material. Toddlers. Children in Hell represent the worst of humanity, and they are downright scary! These are not cute little babes with big eyes that fill with wonder over a simple balloon. These are small children who are weakened by their size and their age, whose faculties have been lessened deem they should start plotting. Their eyes are filled with contempt. They remember who they were, and they remember why they're here. And I can guarantee to anyone who's ever sat with friends and complained that their kids are brats, or ungrateful, or don't listen... there is nothing more terrifying than a Hell-child. They are kept primarily out of the general population. Very rarely we will see one on the street and tend to cross said street before walking by. I've only seen two of them previously. The first time, I averted my eyes as soon as they registered what I was looking at. The fear and the overwhelming sadness I felt when I thought 'who could this have been in life? What terrible things has that now small and pathetic soul accomplished to earn his place among the children of damnation?"

The second one was worse, because I was in one of the discount stores and walked down the wrong aisle to see a full blown tantrum from actual Hell. He was growling, like a beast, deep in his throat as though he was part animal. In his eyes I saw more sheer hatred and despair than I've seen in everyone else in Hell — put together. There was this woman there, I assumed with the boy, who looked absolutely exhausted. She leaned against one of the huge shelving units and started to weep quietly. 'What's worse?' I remember thinking to myself as I turned and left the store immediately, 'To come back as one of those, or to have to take care of it!' For days after I was terrified to go to any store, for fear I would have to come face-to-face with another one of them — another growling, fevered, throwing himself around like a Linda-Blair-in-full-possession-mode demon child.

AND — I almost hit one of the little ankle biters with a giant fucking garbage truck!

Granted, I'm not quite rushing around the truck. I mean, this is a child, and that is the scariest thing I could possibly have to face at any time, let alone after pissing it off. I'm also concerned, since I don't know whether or not I hit it. Like I said, I couldn't have killed it, since it (and all of us) *are* already dead. However, pain is a very real thing down here. Physical and emotional pain are pretty much stock and trade in the Hellverse, so if I hit the kid it's hurt, possibly hurt bad. The good news is, I'm not hearing screaming or crying or an enraged growl, so I'm feeling a little more confident. Then I realize that maybe it's unconscious. Crap. What if there's a bloody knocked-out terror waiting for me on the other side of this truck? I move around so that I can see the street but I'm still provided a certain amount of cover from the vehicle. Just in case I need to run. Believe me, you do not want to be standing directly over that small tornado when it wakes up and realizes it has just been run over and you certainly don't want to be the one that hurt it. But as I turn the corner and take a peek, I gasp at what I see.

It's a girl — a very young girl, maybe 3 or 4 years old. Or, I guess she looks to be 3 or 4 years old. She's blonde with curls that look like she shares a stylist with Little Orphan Annie. She's fully conscious, fully upright, and seems just fine to the naked eye. She's standing on the street wearing this tiny pink denim pair of overalls with a shirt underneath the exact same color of pink but with sparkles on it. She's got a giant red ball and she's bouncing it on the sidewalk and every time it comes back up to greet her tiny little hands she lets out a giggle. It's disarming for a minute as I try to grasp what's happening. The little girl is enjoying herself. Then she looks up into the sky. Eyes wide open, like nothing can hurt her. I would love to be able to look up and see what she sees, but I know I can't because then I'll be blind and in the presence of a Hell-child. That would be right at the top of the list of things you never want to happen to you. But she's still smiling. Could she be mad — bat shit crazy from years and years of being in her own version of torment? But she doesn't seem crazy. She actually seems... well... quite...

Normal. Like a real kid. But that isn't possible for a real child to end up here? Could that happen? No. I refuse to believe that there is anything a child could do that would invoke that kind of wrath. Children are innocent, which is part of the reason (I think anyway) that our worst residents come back as them — to somehow honor the one part of their lives when they were blameless. No, this child does not belong here. My hands are trembling and my palms are damp as I come out from behind the truck. I have no idea what I'm doing, what I'm about to do, or whether I'll be able to do it without peeing my pants.

"Hey Kid!" I say with just a hint of trembling in my voice. "Are you okay?"

The girl turns and looks at me. Inside her eyes I see that she is not of this world. She belongs as far away from Hell as she can get. Inside her blue eyes is wonder... over a simple ball being thrown and bouncing back at her. There are a million questions waiting to be asked, and more. There's something unconditional in those eyes, yet they also seem sad.

"No okay." she says, and begins a small pout. "I want my mommy. I need my mommy!" Her bottom lip starts to tremble — not in a menacing way or an 'I'm about to unleash the tantrum of the century" way, but like a little girl lost and realizing she's far from home.

I walk up to her. "Can I help you find her?" I'm reaching out, hoping she'll take my hand. Where I would take her after that, I don't know. I feel an overwhelming need to get this girl away from here — maybe the agency, Deedy's office, anywhere but here. "Let's go for a ride in my big truck and I'll take you somewhere where you can find her!"

The little girl starts to cry. Not sob, or even cry out loud, but the tears start streaming down her pretty little face. I feel like running and grabbing her, but I can't move. Her tears are like a barrier between us. I'm immobilized by them. "Stop helping me!" she says with childlike anger. It actually makes me smile a little, her indignance. She bounces her ball once more. Then she bounces it toward me. When the red orb reaches my hands, it disappears. I look up, and so has she — vanished — In thin air.

What the fuck? "Kid! Where are you?" Why is everybody vanishing on me today? I can't seem to keep track of a giant Santa, let alone a small helpless child. "Kid??" I walk up the block calling out for her, more and more frantically. She's nowhere. Damn it. All I can do is hope that poor little girl is okay... wherever she is.

As I start to walk back I notice there are full garbage cans lining the street. Isn't that what I'm here for? Okay, so I pick up two of them and haul them to the truck. When I get there I dump them out into the back where it is already half full (don't they dump them out every night? Why would you just haul garbage back to the street where you picked it up the day before?) and see water pouring off of me onto the ground. I wipe my forehead with the intent of getting rid of the fountain of sweat, but my forehead is dry. I take off one of the enormous gloves that I found sitting in the truck and used my bare hand to feel my face. Those salty droplets were not sweat. They were tears. Fuck me if I'm not crying again! I've become such a blat baby lately. I've cried more in the past few days than

I've done in ages.

When I first got here the crying was pretty constant. It's one thing to know that you are dead and will never breathe real air again, or have a real body, or whatever. It's another thing once you realize that you are dead and sentenced to Hell. Sure, there's the standard shock of THAT realization. Hell. The proverbial place where you used to like to tell people to go, or like to joke about going there yourself... but once you find yourself here, well... needless to say those jokes aren't really so damn funny anymore.

But the thing that really gets to you is *knowing* that you are probably alone in this eternal journey. First of all, there is no one... not the very worst person you ever knew in life... not one person that you actually used the word "Hate" to describe... that you would wish here. You certainly wouldn't wish it on anyone you loved. The people I loved, including Linda, would probably end up going in the opposite direction when it's time for them to transition to eternity. I am grateful for that. I'm sincerely glad for them. But that means that I will not get to see them ever. That means that when they make their journey I won't be there to help them along or to stand there with open arms once they arrive.

And of course, that also means that they have a revelation to make once they get where they are going — the realization that I'm not there. I wonder how that would feel? I wonder if there are tears in Heaven? I wonder if anyone there would shed any for me?

81

So anyway, all of that is what helps contribute to the torment of arrival in Hell. That is the reason all of us tend to walk around in a state of teary-eyed delirium for a while. But after a time, who knows how long, all of that starts to meld into a kind of comfort. All the things you knew, the people that made your life worth living, become memories instead of real, live, actual people. There comes a point where you don't even think of them as real anymore. This is good, because the concept that I have them as memories and they will never be down here is the only thing that keeps me functioning.

So why all the new tears now? Maybe it's the whole outrageous experience of meeting Deedy, and Gabby, and the new surroundings in the job. Maybe it's the shock of almost hitting a child, or even seeing a child who looks somewhat normal in this environment. Maybe it's just the overwhelming smell of garbage making me tear up and I should stop analyzing everything.

But I don't think it's any of those things. I felt drawn back to the spot where the little girl disappeared. I feel something about her... her specifically. I feel like I should know who she is, and I should have taken better care of her. I feel an overwhelming sense of guilt when I think about her standing there and looking up at me with those big blue eyes and telling me to "stop helping". I stand at the spot and try to see her again in my mind's eye until the emotions get too heavy for me to bear. I start to cry a bit harder, and I can feel sobs beginning at the base of my gut. When they reach the top I let out just one, then I push it all back, demand it go back in hiding, just for another day or even another moment.

After all, I have work to do.

The cans seem lighter now as I pick them up and start to carry them to my truck.

Is there anything heavier than the burdens we must carry in Hell?

9

I have to say that comparatively speaking, this garbage gig is not the suckiest job I could have down here. Not that I have a lot to compare it to, obviously. My only other job —in death and in life, for that matter — was IP&FW. But other than my overactive imagination that keeps telling me that my arm muscles are screaming under the repetitive strain of picking up cans (and what I've attributed the whole 'little girl' incident to as well), this is really not all that bad. And the best news is that I've gotten through my entire shift with only one pit stop and that was an actual restroom. I'm practically cheerful as I hop in and out of my enormous truck going down street after street. I even see the occasional other person and I almost want to wave, unless they are chasing me down the street cursing at me for coming too early or too late or even on the wrong day. In those cases I usually forgo the wave and replace it with the bird. Nonetheless, all of those things will put me in very good favor with the boss so overall it's a beautiful day in the neighborhood, boys and girls!

In fact, I'm borderline whistling as I turn down the last street on what I think is my route. Of course, I can't be sure since the maps (once I finally dug them out from under the seat) were, as predicted, useless. However, it doesn't matter, because this is the last street I'm doing today regardless.

I park the truck and get out and start hauling the last of the cans for the day when I see an old woman approaching me. She looks like one of the ladies my mom used to have over for cake and coffee after church on Sunday afternoon. Her dress is way too big for her and she's wearing a sweater over it which cannot be the most comfortable thing out here in this heat, but other than that it looks pretty much like an ordinary old lady dress. I remember what Gabby was wearing and I think maybe there's some kind of reward system or something whereby people get less obnoxious clothes over time, or whoever comes up with the nightmare wardrobes each day plays favorites. I also wonder, for the couple of minutes it takes her to make it over to me, what such a sweet-looking old lady could have done to deserve going to Hell. Then of course I start imagining all the horrific things that old ladies can do to go to Hell, recalling everything from a story I once read in a national magazine about a 76 year-old woman who had just buried her 4th husband and an autopsy showed rat poison in his system so they exhumed all of her previous spouses and damned if she hadn't poisoned them all to the fairy tales of my childhood where there was always a sweet old woman who turned out to be a wicked witch eating children or passing out bad apples and I figure 'You know what? It's really none of my business.'

When she finally reaches me, she gives me a smile. I look behind me, just to make sure she's smiling at me and when I surmise that we are the only two people on the street I turn around and smile back. "Morning." I say, trying to sound officious.

"Good Morning! Can I get a hand with some garbage?" she says... not exactly as a question, but polite enough. You know, the way all older people address people younger than they are, as though they are asking for a favor but they understand that of course you are going to do it because they have been on the earth way longer than you, and this is the least you can do for them for living this damn long? That's how she said it. So, obviously I said "Sure thing!" and followed her. I follow her down the street and when she gets to the end she turns the corner.

"Actually, m'am? This street is not on my route. Perhaps someone else is planning to come down here today?" I call after her.

"Right up here!" she says, as if I had asked her where or how far we were going instead of telling her that this address was not in my trash collecting jurisdiction.

So I do the only thing anyone could do under those circumstances — I keep on following her. To her credit, she wasn't lying... it is right around the corner and down a few houses. It's one of the little cutesy houses that the big glass buildings are built around — part of the illusion of a real city within the abyss. On the outside, it looks a bit weather worn (which is part of the illusion, since the only weather down here is fucking hot) and the paint is peeling and the gutters are hanging and there are more than a few shingles missing from the roof. However, none of that general disrepair compares to the backyard. Fenced in, kind of, by a shabby and broken fence that looks like a dotted line, is quite a lot of space that would have constituted a yard. Except, the entire backyard looks like the back of my truck. There are piles and piles of garbage back there.

"I'll need help cleaning this out." says the elderly woman. And I think to myself 'Help? Like how much can this woman be expected to contribute to this process?' I'm thinking that I might have just been shanghaied into spending the next several hours hauling all this to the truck by myself.

"I think the National Guard would need help clearing this place out!" I say and she laughs in response.

"I think if we both put our backs to it, we'll get it done in no time." she says, cheerfully.

How can she be so cheerful? Where does that kind of personal fortitude come from? I wonder again how long she's been here, and what she's done. She seems so normal, and "normal" isn't... well, normal in Hell. I want to ask — to sit at her kitchen table, drink some lemonade, interview her and come away feeling better about being sentenced to eternal anguish. I want to know that, potentially, after a thousand or maybe a million years I'll be able to laugh again. But I know I won't ask a single question. Because to know that this sweet old lady can exist among the iniquitous and vile could mean she's demented, or after a million years we have no choice but to go mad, or possibly it could mean that some folks come here by accident... that would mean the worst thing I could possibly imagine — the creator does not know, or does not care about us once we are down here. That would extinguish the small flame of hope that meeting Deedy and taking this job had lit within me. So I won't ask. Instead, I'll simply say, "Okee doke. Let's get to it. I'm Louise, by the way."

"Thank you Louise. I'm Mrs. Barnes."

Then she started grabbing armfuls of trash and carrying them out. She was actually quite strong, despite her "age". A point that I found a little disquieting after imagining all the terrible things she could have done in life to end up here at the end of it. But she was also just so *nice*... like we were spending the afternoon at a tea party instead of shoveling garbage in Hell.

"So, Mrs. Barnes, what are you going to do with all this space once the trash is gone?" I asked for two reasons. One, I really wanted to know. I mean, as one of the few residents in the 666 area code to actually get some space, I wanted to know what she was going to do with it. And second, we'd been at it for about three hours at this point and had pretty much cleared it all and I just needed a break. So I sat on the curb and looked at her expectantly while she shuffled over to me to answer my question.

She reached into her sweater pocket and pulled out a handful of seeds. I have no idea what kind of seeds, but they were all different. Some were small and wispy like feathers and others were big and bulky. Some were small and round like birdseed and others were flat. "What are the seeds for?" I asked.

"I have no idea!" Her grin was now all the way across her small, wrinkled face. "But I can't wait to see!"

I gave her a slight smile back. "How do you know anything will grow here?"

"I don't. This is what we old folks call a leap of faith."

I wanted to shout at her. 'Leap of faith? Lady, you are in HELL!' But I could hardly bear to look into those cloudy eyes and cause this woman more pain than what she had already suffered. I don't know and never will know what she's guilty of sin-wise to warrant her being down here with fucktards like me. But I do know that my day was better becuase I met her, and I will not take any of her hope away.

"Well then good luck!" I said instead. "With your chrysanthemums or cucumbers or whatever may come up!" I went back to work and quickly helped her clean the rest. Then I climbed into my truck and started to pull away.

"Goodbye Mrs. Barnes! It was very nice to meet you!" I called out the window as I started to leave.

"Goodbye Louise! I hope you are happier today than you were yesterday!" she said and waved as I sat stunned in the drivers' seat of my garbage truck.

Funny. She said the same thing I had said just this morning. Perhaps everyone down here eventually becomes psychic or telepathic or whatever and I just haven't been around long enough. As I'm driving down the street back toward the TCC building I'm thinking about that, and about my first day, and how I actually feel good, better than I've felt I think since I arrived. Then I try to imagine Mrs. Barnes motley garden, with all kinds of flowers growing somewhere that makes no sense. Suddenly, a memory leaps into my mind like a guest at a birthday party jumping out from behind a curtain to yell "Surprise!"

Mr. Comegys and I started our weird morning ritual when I was in high school. I had to walk by his flower stand every day on my way there. Yep, I was one of those kids who walked to school. It wasn't a mile, nor was it uphill both ways. And there was very little snow where I grew up, and when we did get even a powder school was usually cancelled. So this isn't going to be one of those stories.

Anyway, Comegys used to have a big flower shop downtown. When I was a kid I remember going there with my mom to get floral arrangements for church, or a funeral, or something. But when I was in high school I guess he figured there wasn't enough business in Shithole, USA to warrant having a whole entire store, so he closed up shop and put a stand on the corner selling mainly fresh cut flowers.

Bouquets of fresh cut flowers is one thing I will never ever understand. Now, before you start telling me that I was born without the romance gene, let me explain...if some guy wants to actually try to earn my affections he may do so with a number of offerings. Chocolate is always a winner. Making my car payment is good too. But please explain to me what loser was the first one to say "Hey, think I'll go out and cut some living things in assorted colors from their root structure so that they can never absorb enough water or photosynthesize ever again and give them to my girl so she can put them in a fancy jar and watch them decay and die, thereby proving that I love her." And what stupid bimbo was the first girl to respond with this lame gift with "Wow, this is a way better present than something I could keep forever, or maybe eat or drink! I'd much rather have my guy say he loves me with a bunch of flowers that I could, if I were motivated enough, go out and pick myself for free. And the fact that within three days they'll be dried up stalks that I get to throw away is just a bonus!" I hope to meet those two morons one day down here so that I can poke them in the eye for every guy who showed at my door holding a bunch of overpriced roses instead of something sparkly.

Rant aside, I was not born without certain skills, specifically those in the charm department. So, every morning when I would walk by Mr. Comegy's flower stand, he would hand me a single blossom... a rose or a lily, or even the occasional orchid... I'd stop, breathe in the fragrance from the flower and say, "Thank you" to Comegy's with a big grin. He always seemed so pleased with himself so I acted just as pleased. As soon as I got out of eyesight, I'd cut through the graveyard by the Methodist Church and lay the flower on some headstone.

I'd always stop and read the headstone where I laid the flower. Not assessing the person or deciding on who would get the flower, or anything. I'd just pick a headstone at random and before I left I'd take a look to see who had won my own version of the daily lottery. Every once in a while it would be someone I had known, someone who had died within the last 12-18 years who I remembered from the neighborhood or from church or even from school. There was Bruce, this kid I knew from 5th grade who suddenly stopped coming to school. Then a letter came to the entire class from him telling us that he was in a special hospital just for kids. He had enclosed a picture of him sitting in a bed with Ronald Mcdonald next to him and he was surrounded by toys and action figures and stuff that had been given to him. I was horribly jealous of his luck until two weeks later when our principle came in to announce that Bruce had passed away from leukemia. After that, the thought of getting free swag from a celebrity clown didn't seem like such a huge perk. Not in exchange for being dead at age 11. It was sad and we all went to the funeral, and they had grief counselors at school. That was the first time I ever thought about dying. Because he was a kid, like me and now he's gone. His mom took it very hard and she would always stop us classmates on the street whenever she saw us and just sort of look at us with tears in her eyes. I knew that we reminded her of Bruce, and in my childhood ignorance I thought that must be a bad thing. So I would hide - yes hide - from her. I'm not proud of it today, but then I honestly thought I was somehow supplying comfort by not making her cry. When

I realized that I'd set a flower on his headstone I said a silent apology to her, for my childlike ignorance that barred her from a connection with her boy.

Funny, how I've perused so many of my memories from my life since arriving here, hanging on to what I do remember to make up for the fact that I don't remember so much of my later life. Yet, the memory of Comegys was tucked away somewhere and has taken this long to come out and play. Was it the garden and subsequent thoughts of flowers? Was it because I had yet another traumatic day and these memories were a symptom?

With my thoughts a jumble, my arms aching, and emotionally exhausted I pulled into the truck bay at TCC. Evil Santa was waiting for me, clipboard in hand, looking quite officious. I hopped out of the truck and said, "Well boss, I heard the gears grinding a little but I don't think I totally destroyed the truck which is quite an achievement, if I do say so myself!"

He looked at me with this weird face... like part mad, part sad... and said, "Sorry Louise. This isn't gonna work out." Then he handed me a pink slip. An actual pink slip!

"What? What in the fuck are you talking about? I did a fabulous job today!!" My mind is reeling. What could I have done? I was surly, I picked up trash, I almost ran over a kid for fuck's sake. How do you lose a job picking up trash on the first day??

"Oh, yeah you started out really great! We were really jazzed about you in the home office! You were out less than 15 minutes when the phones started ringing with complaints." he stopped to chuckle for a few seconds. "You really know how to piss people off Louise. I would have thought you were born for this job." then he paused. "But then...."

"But then what??" I demanded to know. "Is it because I was kinda nice to Mrs. Barnes?"

"Kind of nice?" Evil Santa says accusingly. "No, it's because you spent 3 hours with her, helping her clean out her yard even after you knew what she was going to do once it was clean!"

"You don't really believe that she is going to be able to grow anything down here do you?" I said, now openly speaking to him like the mentally challenged person I believe him to be. "If I had thought she could possibly get even a weed to sprout up in this shithole I wouldn't have helped. But, knowing she's actively participating in an exercise in futility, I figured, what the Hell? I'll take the garbage... since I've got a GARBAGE TRUCK. And what moron would have given me the keys to a garbage truck if I wasn't supposed to collect trash? So... if we follow that line of thinking to it's obvious and logical conclusion, that would mean YOU, wouldn't it St. Nick? You would be the total fuckin' moron who gave me the keys, then sent me off to pick up trash and now, after one fucking day, is giving me the boot! Well, that is bullshit! And I'll make sure the temp agency knows it!"

Yeah, okay... so all of that is totally not true. I'm actually rooting for Mrs. Barnes and her garden, but I can't let Evil Santa know that and I absolutely, positively, cannot lose my job today. Having to go sit in front of Deedy and tell him I got sacked right out of the gate would be the single worst moment of my entire life. And keep in mind, that once when I was living, I actually got so drunk that I threw up, shit my pants, and passed out all simultaneously. Facing Deedy would feel worse than that. I have to try and save this crappy job if I possibly can.

Evil Santa starts laughing again. "Yep Louise, you sure know how to piss people off. Sorry." Then he forces me to accept the pink slip. I look down at it and read with tears welling up in my eyes:

Termination for Inciting Hope

10

As I walked back to the agency I'm vacillating between total rage, panic, and humiliation. First, I'm just plain pissed off. The reason I took this crazy temp job gig is because the agency implied (though they never came out and said... hmmmmm....) that there might be some loophole that I could use to get out of here. To go where, I don't know, but anywhere is better than here, right? I mean, let's look at the choices: Purgatory — that's a possibility. Sitting around in nothingness hoping someone will pray me into heaven. However, considering the fact that I'm not, and never have been Catholic (I didn't even have a lot of Catholic friends. There was Molly O'Brien in elementary school who was a good friend of mine. But after my first sleepover at her house the combination of my giggling at the dinner table when they crossed themselves, and sneaking her dad's cigarettes after her parents went to bed... well, suffice it to say Molly turned green after 3 puffs of a Camel unfiltered and we started a small fire in the living room which pretty much put the kibosh on the two of us ever hanging out again.) means I'm probably not on the "Will Call" list at the Purgatory Club.

Then there's the whole reincarnation question. Could it be? Could I just be sent back to do it all over again like a giant mulligan? Whoa, that's an interesting concept. Unless... I could be sent back and end up in one of those third-world countries where celebrities are always going to get their pictures taken with the poor and wretched children. Those kids always have flies landing on their lips and pathetic shit like that. This particular option would suck. You know, partially because I probably wouldn't even know that the people getting their pictures taken with me were famous, since I more than likely wouldn't even know what a television is, and partially because of the whole "fly landing on lips" thing.

The last option? Well, I can't really think about the last option. I mean, really... could there be a place in H-town for someone whose eternity has already been deemed fire and brimstone worthy? And let's say there was a way to actually earn a place in Heaven from Hell? How could it be earned or proven unless the person in question showed a certain capacity for compassion or the ability to do good? Okay, and HOW in the name of everything sacred, is a person supposed to do that if every time this person does anything even remotely redeemable - BOOM - down comes the hammer right smack dab on her damn head??

This is where the panic sets in. What if this was my only chance? What will happen when Deedy finds out I got fired right away? What happens if he gives me one of those wise smiles of his, maybe pats me on the back (probably not though, considering that whole no touch policy of his), and tells me not to let the door hit me in the ass on my way out. What if I have, in fact, destroyed any possibility of a second chance? But my real fear? In my heart of hearts my actual fear is that I might end up exiled from the agency… from Deedy. Mr. Deedy, the man who seems to know me better than I know myself. Mr. Deedy, the man with the fabulous suit in a world where clothing is punitive, not to mention office furniture, and the best assistant in town. Mr. Deedy, whose company has quickly, yet completely, become something that means more to me than I can even bear to describe here.

That cues the tears, along with the crushing humiliation that comes with the knowledge I may have disappointed the only truly important person I've met since the day I passed away.

I pause in front of the doors to the agency to check myself in the reflective glass and try to pull myself together. Also, I haven't forgotten Gabby's special gifts, so I'm also trying to collect my thoughts and make them somewhat non-incriminating for the mind reader. I'm trying desperately to give myself a pep-talk, not wanting to dissolve into a giant, wet, snotty mess the second I get upstairs. Once I feel like I've gotten my poop in a group, I reach for door only to have a uniformed arm reach out from behind me and open the door for me.

"Will!" I say excitedly as I turn to face his boyish smile. He's back in his Monkey Suit. "How did you change so quickly? Did you pull a Hepburn in the back of a cab?"

He looks at me with a confused look on his face. I can't help but smile, no matter how awful I feel inside. "So, not a *Breakfast at Tiffany's* fan?" I say teasingly.

He looks at me and laughs as we make our way across the lobby, once again arm in arm. "Actually I have had plenty of time. After I left you this morning I was able to make my way over here. You just caught me coming back from running a few errands for the Boss."

I draw my breath in as though I've been struck. Not only at the mention of "the Boss" but also if he left that early than Will must not know. So, I look at him and said "You haven't heard, then?"

"That you were let go? Yeah, I heard. And I'm sorry Louise. Really." he looks at me with sincere sympathy. "So is that where you are headed? Upstairs to tell the Boss?"

"Trying to work up the nerve, to be honest. Or maybe waiting for some inspiration to strike that will give me a great excuse for not being able to go longer than a day on my first assignment." I say, all of the sudden feeling dejected again.

"Want some advice from a relatively new 'old friend'?" he says.

"Sure." At this point, I would take anything.

"Just tell him the truth. Speak from the heart. It's not like he won't know anyway if you are lying. Surely you've already figured that out about him."

"Yeah, he's definitely got a highly tuned bullshit meter." I say with a sigh. "Will, do you know anything about him? Why he is here? Why his office is so comfortable? Why his clothes don't look like a bad practical joke?"

Will laughs and says "Louise, I'm just a paltry elevator guy. Those are all worthwhile questions though — questions for him, however. Not me."

"Thanks Will, for everything today. Without you I probably wouldn't have lasted the few hours I did."

He gave me a small bow and pats me on the arm again. "You'll be just fine. Come My Lady, your chariot awaits!" he says just as the doors open — the doors to my elevator of doom.

When they open again, I'm on the 17th floor. I find myself once again frozen, my legs apparently turning slowly into spaghetti before my very eyes. The funny thing is, this time it is not the height that has me all bugged out, it's what's waiting for me inside. I realize that right at the moment I know exactly how a murderer feels when he walks into the execution chamber.

"Are you going to join us today Louise? Or did you just come to play on the elevator?" says Gabby from inside. It's enough to make my spaghetti legs snap to attention. I step off to find her standing there smiling. And in her hand is a steaming cup of that glorious coffee. I take it gratefully.

"This might be my last cup of this wonderful coffee, Gabby." I say, savoring each and every sip.

"Why would you think that, dear?" she says

"I can't bear to tell the story twice, so you'll have to get the highlights later. Is he in?" I say.

"In and waiting for you." she replies "Go on... You'll be fine." Weird, isn't that verbatim what Will said to me on the elevator?

I walk toward the office with my spaghetti legs slowly turning to something more in the lead category. When I get to the door I pause, steel myself, and quietly say 'Do not fall apart. Do not fall apart. Do not fall apart."

Then I walk through the door and fall apart.

Deedy is sitting behind his desk holding up a check in front of his face with his smiling eyes peeking over it. "Bore-Da Louise Patterson!" he exclaims, apparently in his native tongue, and he looks so happy for me I just can't help but cry. Suddenly his face changes to one of concern.

"My darling girl, I thought you'd be more pleased... what with this being your first check from the agency!"

I actually start to sob now. "Yeah well, you'd better keep it. In fact, put in it in the curse jar. Because I'm in no condition to watch my language." I can literally feel the snot building up inside my head. This is not going to be pretty.

"Oh my." says Deedy, with nothing but concern in his voice. "You'd better tell me everything."

I sink into one of his comfy chairs, trying to imprint the feeling onto my brain since it may be the last time I get to sit in one for all of time itself. "I will..." I start, knowing that I will tell him about the little girl, and the spooky way she was there and then wasn't, and about Mrs. Barnes and her crazy potluck garden, and about how I felt when I saw Will there, and about Evil Santa, and driving the truck. But there's one thing I have to get off my chest first, so I say "But first, I have to start at the end. I... got... fucking... fired!"

Then I just start to wail.

11

At last I'm lying in my bed after another long and emotional day. Long and emotional are my new M.O. much to my own chagrin. However, Deedy let me talk and talk, which I have to admit makes the new soppy me a little easier to bear. Deedy sat patiently, in another gorgeous suit by the way, while I regaled him with tales of my day. He didn't even flinch when I occasionally forgot myself and let rip a four letter word or two (or seven or ten...). He laughed out loud at my reproach of Evil Santa after he copped a feel, and had the good graces to look slightly embarrassed when I shared the fact I had discovered Will there to watch over me.

We talked about Mrs. Barnes and her unlikely garden and the idea of this poor old woman planting mystery seeds in the single most hostile environment ever known seemed to delight him beyond all reason. However, even that couldn't compare to Deedy's excitement over my story about Comegy's flower stand.

"And what did you learn about yourself with that uncovered memory?" he asked me.

"I learned... that... even girls that claim to hate flowers are incapable of saying no to a man that has one in his hand?"

Deedy laughed at that. "I'm sure you must have discovered something else. Something about your own nature?" He stared at me with those endlessly patient eyes.

"I guess so. I guess this means that I'm kind of nice! I mean, it was nice of me to take the flower every day. Oh! And putting it on graves, right? That made me nice too! It was a good deed kind of thing." I'd always heard good deeds wouldn't get you into heaven. Maybe I was wrong, and maybe with a few more memories like this I'll be home free.

Deedy chuckled. "It's not about nice, Louise." I figured that was too easy. "It is about respect. It is about the regard in which you held Mr. Comegys, by never wanting to bring him discomfort by refusing his daily gift. And yes, it was about the graves too. About the very indiscriminate, yet unbelievably considerate way you chose to use that gift. To place it on a grave and to pay your respects to the person it represented regardless of whether you knew the person or how that person had lived. You never asked whether she was good enough, or made enough money, or whether he was handsome enough. You never asked if she cheated on her husband or did he beat his wife? You just left a blessing on a random grave, and in return you were blessed."

Those three words. "You were Blessed" was enough to make the tears flow freely once again. "I swear, I wasn't anything like this in life. I just want you to know." I said, as I wiped some bawling-inspired mucus onto the sleeve of that hideous orange jumpsuit.

"Like what, darling girl?" Deedy asked as he tugged on his perfectly tailored sleeve, then reached into his desk for a box of tissues in response.

"This emotional — I didn't burst into tears every time I saw a puppy or a really great greeting card commercial." I said with disdain.

"Well..." Deedy said thoughtfully "It's been a rough eternity for you so far."

That made me actually giggle a little. Good old Deedy, the only person I've ever met that could make someone smile while literally walking through Hell.

But then I told him about the little girl. He almost jumped out of his seat.

"Tell me about her."

I told him about what she was wearing, about the ball, about how adorable she was. How frightened I was when I thought I'd hit her, and how she disappeared.

"Can you tell me her name, Louise?" he asked.

"No. She never told me." I answered. That's a weird question, right? I mean, a little girl shows up in the middle of Hell and all Deedy wants to know is her name?

"Okay. Well, overall Ms. Patterson. I'd say your first day at the agency was a resounding success!" Deedy said, in his game show host voice.

"Grand success? I got FIRED Deedy." I answered. "Eh, it's a process." he replied. "You'll get the hang of it. Now here's what I really need to know. How did you feel about the whole driving thing?"

"It was actually kinda cool." I said, with a just a bit of pride in my voice. "Having to control that big old truck, it was the closest thing to fun I've had since I got here."

"Good. Because driving is the only skill set you need for your next assignment! And of course, I'm saying that half jokingly. Since the worse your driving skills are, the more successful you're going to be!" Deedy passes me another piece of paper. "Welcome to the world of hired transport, my darling girl!"

Another assignment! And as a cabbie! I was so excited I almost leaped across that big desk and hugged Deedy, if it hadn't been for knowing that even the concept of doing such a thing would horrify him in every conceivable way. "Thank you Mr. Deedy. Thank you, thank you, thank you!"

My enthusiasm made him smile. "Now go, and get some sleep. You have to be alert tomorrow."

As I started to leave, I remembered I had a few questions about him, and who or what he was. I turned and Deedy was starting straight at me, like he knew what I was about to say. "Can I just ask..." I started, when he put up a long, elegant hand.

"Not yet, darling girl... not yet," was all he said.

And, for whatever reason, that was just fine with me.

Tonight sleep creeps onto me slowly, which makes the veil between reality and dreams get blurred and thin. These dreams feel real, and vivid, and nightmarish. The fear is especially real, as if it's in own separate character in the nightmare. I hate these dreams.

I'm in a house. It's an absolutely huge house with an elevator. I'm pretty sure I've never been in a house big enough for an elevator, however I seem to be quite used to it in nightmare world. The house seems really run down and in disrepair, which means that the elevator doesn't work all the time. I find myself wandering around, crawling through ducts, going up and down endless staircases. That's the part that I hate the most. Nightmares are even more frightening sometimes than Hell itself. Even in Hell everything has a sense of reason, time is still kinda linear, and even the supernatural bullshit comes from such an obvious perspective that you would have to be blind not to see it coming. The thing is that tonight, as it is most of the time, the dream version of me never stops and says "This fucking house makes no sense!!" The dream 'me' just gets more and more panicked as I keep getting more and more lost.

I get to the point where I can barely breathe with fear and something else... the sense of being alone and knowing that I shouldn't be. Who else should be here? Linda? Mom and Dad? Is this supposed to be my house? These are passing thoughts that don't actually enter my dream mind but float above it like a voice from above.

Here's the thing... what are nightmares but the subconscious mind exploring the things that we most fear? And what is there to fear in life? Well, pretty much everything including the final and all encompassing fear of dying. But if you are already dead, than what is there to fear? People would assume that death means the ultimate freedom from anything frightening, but they would be very, very wrong. I can't exactly say it in words... but I can tell you that it scares the shit out of everyone down here. And whatever it is, I feel it tonight in this dream house. I feel it breathing down my neck, waiting to pounce on me. Waiting inside my aloneness. Perhaps that is it, Loneliness personified, and what could be more terrifying than that? So I keep on running through the corridors and ductwork searching for the something or someone that will bring me peace, even as I realize that I have no idea who that may be.

Suddenly I find myself on a staircase standing on a landing at the top looking across a large foyer over to the other side where there's an identical staircase. Standing on that staircase is the little girl — the same little girl from the trash truck incident. I feel that same wave of affection and familiarity as I recognize her. She's smiling now, unlike the last time I saw her when her adorable face was contorted with anger. I smile back and wave at her. She squeals, like she's actually happy to see me. Then she says, "You found us!" and claps her hands in pure, childlike joy. "I'm very relieved to see you again. You scared me when you dashed off from my garbage truck!" I started to say, with just a mild tone of scolding. Then I realized she said 'us'. "Do you have someone with you sweetie?" All of the sudden he appeared behind her... an absolutely gorgeous man — average height, not average build. More like a brick shithouse, with muscles straining against the seams of a black tee shirt. Dark, wavy hair that is cut short, as if he's trying to make it submit yet it's still just a little wild. His skin is golden, just tan enough without making him look like he spends too much time in a tanning bed. His strong, sinewy arms are encircled around the girl's shoulders, and when his glance darts from her to me, I find myself staring into the most beautiful blue eyes I've ever experienced, smiling at me from behind wire rimmed glasses. I feel my breath draw in quickly as I return his gaze. Then I notice him looking again at my small, strange friend. There's a sense of familiarity they display toward one another. Maybe they are related? Maybe he's her protector in the afterlife? I am aware that there are so many things running through my head. First, I'm hoping against hope that this precious girl is not dead, that she's just a figment of my warped imagination. Second, I wish upon every star that I will never see again that I could feel that protection, that kind of devotion, to have strong arms to wrap around me and take away all the fear in this horrible house, or maybe even from Hell itself.

Finally, and the one thought that leaves me feeling cold as it drills into my brain is what if I am what's waiting in the darkness, the unknown demon that sneaks around in the black and makes the hair on the back of your neck stand up? What if the handsome man is protecting the little girl from me?

I bolt awake and sit upright in my bed. Nightmares suck. My head is pounding with images from my dream still banging around up there. I sit in the stillness for a moment and recall the faces that had been real to me just a few minutes before. Why is this little girl suddenly everywhere? Is she a lesson I'm supposed to learn? Is she a symbol? Is she my inner child who can't be kept inside anymore? And the man with her — what a man! Kudos to my imagination for coming up with something like him. However, no matter how lovely he was, how blue those eyes were there was a certain sadness in them. It's a realization that chills me now even in the bright light and heat of the day.

Who are these ghosts that haunt the dead instead of the living? And why are they haunting me?

Okay, so speaking of the heat of the day, it's time to shake off the horrors of the dark and get to work. Today I get to be a cab driver! That concept might create some anxiety inside of me if I were living, since I rarely go unescorted beyond the three or four blocks of my own address, mainly because I was born without that internal compass everyone else in the universe apparently has inside their brains. My complete lack of a sense of direction is still a source of amusement in some circles. When I turned sixteen and got my driver's license, my mom said she would send me to the store and never see me again. Of course, she was eating those words when I turned thirty and was still sponging off her. However, in Hell, the thought of me being responsible for getting people places, particularly on time, spawns anticipation instead of fear. Because here cabbies don't ever know where they are going and they never get you there on time. The only reason every cab ride in Hell doesn't end with a fiery crash and a huge body count is primarily because we are all already dead and, metaphorically at least, already on fire.

Cab drivers don't wear uniforms. The fact that I'll be inside of a metal box with a choice between no climate control or spasmodic blasts of even more heat is a little worrisome.

Whatever the closet prepares for me today, I sure hope it is something a little breathable. That thought is bouncing around in my head as I approach the portal to my daily torture chamber — a.k.a. my closet. Then, as I open the door, I realize that I should never think thoughts like that as I am opening anything in Hell, because it had obviously read my mind and produced the diametric opposite of my wish. This is an absolute testimony to the bottomless cruelty and the punitive irony, and just a bit of sardonic humor that whoever is in charge of this process must have in spades because there it is... FUCKING LEATHER.

First of all, as everyone knows, leather does not breathe — at all. It absorbs heat and multiplies it and turns it into a smelly liquid form that then coats every nook and cranny of your body. Leather is bad. And down here, leather is tragic. I don't even want to know what the inside of my cab is going to smell like at the end of the day.

And secondly, leather should never, ever be worn by anyone over the age of thirty for any reason whatsoever. Hear me living people? Take notes on this. My sorry tale may turn out to be the greatest lesson some poor sap may ever learn. But if you learn nothing from my pathetic life, learn this... stop wearing leather! Now, a leather jacket is fine, and that is a classic look that almost anyone can pull off. And a leather vest? Maybe. Particularly if you ride a motorcycle or want people to think that you do. Leather skirts? Only if the time/space continuum has a glitch and it becomes permanently 1987. But leather pants? Absolutely not. Leather pants are a privilege people! Something you must be young and thin to enjoy. Unless you are Steven Tyler (and even he was starting to look a bit ridiculous in them when I left the planet), take the leather pants the fuck off.

Having said that, it's time to put mine on. I hate this place.

After spending an extraordinary amount of time trying to pull on a pair of leather pants in broiling heat, I finally leave my apartment winded and pissed off. Despite that, and the nagging sensation of impending exhaustion from last night's nightmare marathon, I'm feeling pretty positive about today. Today should be tremendously successful by Hellion standards. And no one needs to worry about me accidentally helping someone or inciting any unnecessary hope because today my mood is pretty much black enough to make me feel almost qualified to be a cab driver in Hell.

I follow the directions to the dispatch office of the cab company printed on the small post-it Deedy had given me. This time, wiser and more jaded than I was during my first temp experience, my eyes are peeled the whole way there looking for Will and his sneaky, spying self. Just as I am approaching the dispatch bay, I see him ducking behind a gas pump. I walk past and say, "Watch out Will, huffing those fumes will give you a killer migraine. Ask me how I know," and keep on walking laughing out loud.

Thanks to the Second Chance Temp Agency, I've laughed and cried more in the past few days than I would have thought possible just a few weeks ago.

I walk into the tiny glass enclosed office within the car bay. The smell of gasoline and oil is thick in the air, and with the heat it seems like another person inside the garage with me — like a new, stinky imaginary friend. It looks like they have about six or seven cabs — not nearly enough for the size of Hell. However, since the idea of having plenty of cabs in Hell is borderline ridiculous, and you'd have to be brain damaged or new to actually ride in one, it really shouldn't be a surprise.

I walk into the office and expect to see a diminutive man with a cigar and a temper like Danny Devito in Taxi. Instead, I find myself face to face with a GIANT. I mean an actual giant person straight from central casting for the latest fairy tale movie! This guy is HUGE — big broad shoulders that have to span at least four feet. He is so tall that even though we're in a decent sized office, he has to kind of stoop over when he stands or he'll hit his head. And he's got the largest feet I've ever seen. I can hear Linda's voice in my head saying revolting things about the probable size of the rest of his anatomy based on those clown-shoe sized feet and I can't help but glance at his waist for a teensy minute.

He lumbers from behind the desk and comes toward me with a grin that is proportionate to the rest of his body. His teeth are atrocious. Gaps where some are missing, others just black and rotting in his head, and others are just yellowed with age and stains. He's wearing a pair of ordinary jeans, which is kind of surprising, although they are quite short and fall well above his ankles. However, considering he's got to be almost 7 feet tall I can only imagine these are probably very similar to what he wore in life. His shirt is a little juvenile. A tee shirt with a childhood cartoon character on it. And it's kind of feminine. I search my memory banks for a name of this cartoon. It's something-something-bears. With colorful stuffed bears with rainbows and shit plastered on the front of them. His is kind of lavender. At any rate, humiliating yes, but uncomfortable? No. He grasps my hand and his enormous hand envelopes mine until you can no longer see it. I am literally quite frightened for a moment or two that I may pull back a stump where my hand used to be. He pumps my hand with great enthusiasm and says, "You must be Louise! I'm Tim. I'm so happy to make your acquaintance!" He says it kind of slowly and very deliberately. I shudder as I imagine why he's found himself here — in this horrible place. I get snatches of "Of Mice and Men" and wonder if he accidentally hurt someone. But if it had been an accident, he wouldn't have ended up here right? I disengage my hand from him and weakly return his smile. "Thanks," I reply. "Ready to get to work!"

"Okee dokey!" He says again with a huge grin. "We've got three cabs to choose from. One is pretty beat up, it used to be Carl's. He liked to take customers right up to the door. Occasionally he took customers THROUGH the door," Tim pauses for single beat then bursts into laughter at his own joke. After a minute of that, he wipes a laughter induced tear out of the corner of his eye and continues, "The other two just arrived. I don't know where they come from, but I think it might be from the same place where you got that outfit," again with the pause only this time long enough to give me a sorrowful look, as if he's finding my fucked-up closet choice more pitiable than his! Harumph! "So no guarantees, sorry."

"Fine," I say, with just a touch of an offended tone, due to the whole 'poor little Louise stuck in leather' look. "I will happily take one of the new ones out for a test drive!" I didn't bother to even ask what happened to Carl, since I figured he wouldn't tell me anyway and I was terrified of the possible answers. The biggest one being that Carl was fired, which would set precedent that it is possible for a person to actually get fired as a cab driver. And my track record is two for two on the whole getting shitcanned thing.

"Good for you!" Tim says, with just a hint of condescension. I'm really not sure whether to like Tim, to pity him, or to punch him in the throat. It's a strange conflict. He does make me feel just a wee bit anxious and very uncomfortable over his actual presence here. We all believe that there are some basic rules, and those rules help us make sense of the world around us, even if that world is this one. A week ago I would have said with all the confidence in the universe that there were no innocent children in Hell, but then my new little blonde friend started appearing. And I would have asserted that if you're slow or mentally challenged, you're pretty much guaranteed a ticket to a penthouse in the afterlife. But here's Tim with his gappy smile and his overly concerned looks regarding my wardrobe and now I don't know what to think. With a shudder, I decide to stop thinking and just go to work already.

"Thanks Tim. Got the keys?"

"Yup," he says and goes back to his desk. He grabs a set of keys with a large "3" on the keyring and tosses them over to me. "Be careful out there, kiddo," he says with a hint of sincere concern. I immediately regret considering hitting him. He walks up to me and places one of his giant hands on my shoulder. I look up and into his eyes and again I am overwhelmed by a wave of discomfort. His eyes are so kind. It's not just hard, it's damn near impossible to believe that he could have done anything to warrant being damned for eternity.

"I mean it. It gets rough out there. Don't let it get to you," he says. Then he pats my shoulder a couple of times and turns his back to me.

I swear, as I'm heading out of his office toward bay three for my cab, I can hear him sniffle as if he's crying. I wonder for a moment if he's crying over his own fate or if he's crying for me.

As soon as I get inside my car I feel at home. In the world of breathers and breeders, I never cared about my car. I had a drivers license and occasionally I even had a car, but it was usually a piece of shit beater car that I used simply to get from point A to point B. I never understood people who named their car or took photos of their car and framed them or spent more on their car payment than my parents did on their first mortgage. I thought of my car as a tool, an occasional place to sleep or fuck if there was absolutely no alternative. But my car was never an extension of myself. So I never got people, especially men, who had a more intimate relationship with their transportation than they had with wives, mistresses, or children.

But that was then. This is now. And today I get it. Because after working at a call center in a teensy weensy cubicle that looks exactly like the 42 others on either side of it, I understand why people feel at home when they are in a car. It's like sacred space, small enough to feel intimate and everything adjusts to fit you — just you. I adjusted all the mirrors and the seat. I wish I had something really personal and me-like to hang from the rear view mirror. I'm wondering if the radio works and I'm about to try it when the smaller, cb-like radio below it goes nuts. I hear Tim's slow-speaking tone come over and say "cab 3, cab 3, Louise, you out there?" "Tim, I'm directly in front of your office in the car bay!" "Oh good... wait a second," he said and then his giant head popped up from nowhere in the window. He gives me a great big smile and a wave then disappears again.

"Did ya see me?" he says with an obvious smile.

"Of course I did!" I say laughing.

"Okay, well I have your first pick up. It's on Moss Ave and 3rd Street."

"Okee doke. Is there a map or something in here?" I say looking around.

"Nope. Sorry." He says.

"Not a problem!" I say and back out of the bay with a huge grin.

This job should be a cake walk.

So here I am. Driving around like a maniac, not even caring which direction I'm going with a guy in the back seat screaming like I'm torturing his mother or something. It took me about 45 minutes to find the address where I picked him up, so he was pretty pissed off by the time I pulled up and gave him my best winning smile. He got in the car and starting blathering on about needing my corporate office's number as well as taking down my tag number and screaming about how he was going to be contacting them to complain. So, I'm thinking he's real new in town. And I'm thinking I might just earn a promotion or something on my first day as a cabbie. This job fucking rocks like The Who, baby!

I notice, with just a twinge of disappointment, that his destination is right ahead. I have to brake pretty hard to stop within a block past it and the guy literally leaps out of the cab and runs behind me screaming. I pull away chuckling and and thinking to myself that I just might be able to make the next guy boot if I try really hard. But then I'd be stuck in a car that has no working air conditioning and smells like vomit. So maybe that is not such a brilliant idea.

I get on the radio and call Tim. "Dropped off my first fare. Ready for the next one!" I say with great enthusiasm.

"Good Job Louise!" Tim answers with equal, if not greater enthusiasm. "You are a natural at this!" he says with a bit of awe in his slow speech. You just gotta love Tim. Then he comes back on the radio with my next fare — approximately ten minutes from here unless I take the long way around, which of course I am because I'm that committed to being successful at something down here in Hades. And it's fun.

So I turn the corner toward the left (my fare is to the right) just in time to catch a view of something that sends my mind reeling and sets my foot directly on the brake — a red ball bouncing around the corner up a block. I can't see who's behind that ball, but I have a clue. I wait with breathless anticipation as the ball turns the corner and the bouncer comes into view.

Yep. It's her. The same little blond girl that I am now convinced is here solely to drive me over the edge of my sanity. A hellish vision of something seemingly normal and innocent to make me question my own eyes and what little is left of my earthly brain.

Why is she here? Why am I suddenly seeing her? Her appearances are becoming more frequent and yes, I've already put it together that her sudden entrance into Hell coincides with my working for Deedy. But I still don't understand what she is supposed to be telling me, or making me do, or whatever. I'm not even sure she is actually here. No one else seems to see her. People walking down the streets of Hades should be staring at a blonde smiling child bouncing a ball down the street the same way breathers back on Earth would stare at an alien walking down the street bouncing a head or something. Yet she gets no reaction from anyone, which leads me to believe that she is here solely for me — or a hallucination. Can you have acid flashbacks in the afterlife? That thought is actually enough to distract me for a minute and I almost lose the little girl. I swerve around a moon-crater sized pothole and pull over (actually, pull up on the curb) and jump out of the car. I sprint down the block and around the next corner where she has already bounced her pretty ball and ringlet curls around.

"Kid!" I say breathlessly as I stoop over to try and get more oxygen in my unfit (and also imaginary) lungs.

She stops bouncing and looks at me quizzically. Then she looks behind her as only as a child could, or would for that matter. She bends over backwards and tilts her head all the way in the other direction so that she's looking at the world upside down. I laugh at the sight of her. I can imagine me doing that when I was her age. Actually I can imagine me doing that at pretty much any point in my life, but I'm pretty sure I would not have been that adorable when I did it.

"Hey! Found her!" she yells behind her and then stands upright and gets a small rush to her head. You can see the dizziness pass through her eyes immediately followed by a wide smile and a sparkle of sheer delight in her eyes. Good grief. This kid is fucking hilarious.

"Do not get too attached to that feeling," I say. "Because when you get older it will become more difficult to get. Just say no, right?" Her response is a precious giggle.

I'm so busy looking at this little girl and enjoying all the cuteness that I don't see the man abruptly come behind her. I hear him before I see him. "Hey Weez." he says, with a twinge of intimacy that gives me chills.

"Hey," I say back. I have no idea what else to say.

I look up and once again I am faced with the most perfect pair of eyes ever created — bluest blue, and so kind. His eyes smile before the rest of his incredibly gorgeous face. This is the beautiful man from my nightmare last night. How could I have seen him in my dream before actually meeting him? Of course, if he's a hallucination than he's from my brain anyway so the whole chicken before the egg question is moot — since it's all eggs and it's getting more scrambled by the minute.

I stand up very straight, and stick out my chest. This is a hardwired thing that I always do when I'm faced with a hottie. It's like Pavlov's dog experiment. He looks kind of geeky, with the glasses and the hair. But it's geeky in a "sexy male librarian in a porn movie" kind of a way. He is looking at me too, yet not at my breasts, which I am basically presenting him like something on Mutual of Omaha's Wild Kingdom. Instead he's looking directly into my eyes.

"So tell me Weez, are you happier today than you were yesterday?" he asks.

"Probably, if I'm being honest, but I don't think all of my tomorrows are going to be wonderful," I say back sweeping my arm around to take in my environment. So this little idiom must be a thing with me.

He laughs in response. "I will say this, for a Weasel you sure are pretty."

A weasel? This guy is a total stranger and he just called me a rodent. I think. I'm not exactly sure what species the Weasel falls under, but whatever it is, being called one is probably not a compliment. So why am I smiling? And why do I feel this tremendous warmth toward this strange and beautiful man and his little girl?

"Well," I say teasingly, "I may be a weasel, but you are not going to get any points as a body guard or baby sitter if you keep letting little Princess here wander around Hell all by herself!"

He smiled a sad smile at me that once again landed on the back of my neck like a pair of ghostly lips. I actually shudder. Then he says "We're just waiting."

"For what?" I say as he casually puts his arm on the little girl's and guides her in the opposite direction of me. I will admit, watching him walk away is almost as good as him standing right in front of me, but he doesn't answer my question.

"Hey you! Pretty boy!" I yell after him. He just holds up his hand and waves as they turn the next corner, and once again disappear.

Okay, so back in the car and to my next fare. If I were a cab driver in the world of the living, I may be too distracted to drive people around today. But for now, I think I will be fine. I slow down to a crawling pace to pick up the poor schmuck who has been waiting now for over an hour. I expect him to jump in the car and go directly for my throat, but no such luck. This guy is a walking ad for Prozac.

I assume he's a newbie. New arrivals tend to either be furious that they ended up here or they just weep for days or weeks or months. This guy is one of the latter. He jumps in the backseat and blows his nose on the sleeve of his burgundy velveteen jacket, which, by the way, is paired with trousers so orange they look like you could juice them. Under the jacket is a wooly turtleneck that makes me itch just to look at it. He's young. Looks like he's in his early twenties and with his red swollen eyes and those little snot bubbles coming from his nostrils, he looks even younger. This guy reeks of pathetic anguish.

"Where to buddy?" I ask in my best cabbie voice.

"How do you know my name?" he asks with a genuine touch of surprise.

"I don't... or didn't, Sherlock. Surely you've been called 'Buddy' by strangers before? And seriously? You're real name is Buddy?"

"Yes to the name question and no to the other one. I didn't actually meet a lot of people before I..." he crumples into despondent sobs before he can say the word *dies*. That is a tough word to say when you are actually in it.

"So you're a small town guy too? I was from Shithole, USA myself." I am now trying to make small talk. Aren't I an awesome cab driver?

"Funnily enough, no," He says through tears, and not just a little bit of snot. "I was born and raised in Brooklyn. But I had a very religious mother. Well, she was fanatical. I think if we actually knew any of our neighbors they would have called child services and saved me from a life of torment."

Crap. My small talk skills need massaging.

"Sorry about all that. I just need to know where you want to go?" I ask, trying to get this back on track.

"Where would I like to go?" he says wistfully as he takes another swipe of his endlessly seeping nose with his sleeve. "I would like to go to school. Instead of being home schooled by a woman who believes that William fucking Shakespeare was one of those liberal homosexuals with an agenda to promote cross-dressing and molesting young boys while he wrote filthy pornography to display in front of the unwashed masses. Or that the theory of evolution is a plot by the Jews to snuff out the one true faith! And don't even get me started on what she thinks of math, or poetry, or any of the core subjects that any person should know if they are to become a productive member of society. And computers? Do you know that I was seventeen fucking years old before she'd even allow a computer in the house? And then only because the Good Reverend Barker from the God's Way Television Network decided to get himself a website complete with prayer lists and the ability to make donations from the comfort of your own home with a debit or credit card! I had to wait until she was asleep so that I could get online and give myself some facsimile of a reasonable education!"

Holy shit. This guy has some issues. However, I'm driving a cab, not operating a confessional.

"Well, you do seem kinda smart," I say, trying to be nice.

"Kinda? I have an IQ of over 170! I could have written my own ticket. MIT, Harvard, Yale, anywhere! Even with a public school education. But no, public schools have dances and dances are just fronts for teenage girls giving each other abortions in the restrooms while the boys gang rape the hormonally charged prostitutes that the state hires to be teachers. That, by the way, is a direct quote."

If it wasn't so terrible, it would be kind of funny.

"Wow. But you know, everyone thinks their Mom is crazy...." I said. Bad thing to say — real bad. It would probably be best if I stopped talking altogether.

"Crazy Mom? No. Crazy Mom tells you that you look thin even though you are thirty pounds overweight and she cooks enough food to feed a small country and expects you to eat it. Crazy Mom collects little cartoon frogs and places them on shelves all over the house. Crazy Mom buys you ugly sweaters every Christmas from QVC and makes you wear them out in public. Crazy Mom may be exasperating but you always know she loves you." Buddy is now in full blown rant mode, and I need help. I start looking down the curb hoping someone, anyone, will show up and try to hail me down. I see her ahead. A woman who looks about thirty-five but dressed like she's seventy-five in a dull, gray polyester suit with a skirt that falls to her shins is standing just ahead us of with a panicked look on her face. With Buddy still screaming in the backseat, I pull off to the side until I'm directly in front of her. I lean over and open the passenger side door and say (over the sobbing rants of the mad man in the back) "Hey, need a ride somewhere?"

She looks down and heaves a sigh of relief. "Would I!" and lets herself in the back where Buddy is now coming to a crescendo of anger and bile. "...but my horrific bitch of a mother never, ever made me feel anything but shame and guilt, as if I had asked to be born or was some sort of punishment brought down upon her by her angry, vengeful God!" "Okay Buddy, now it's time to ride quietly and share the cab with this nice lady," I said. I realized I was talking to him like a five year old instead of the genius he apparently is, but I don't care. I'm getting a headache.
"That's okay. I don't mind. I used to be a psychologist in the world. I'm Hazel, and your name is?" she says to Buddy while she offers her hand.

Buddy looks a little terrified of this female hand in front of him. He turns into one of those beaten dogs you can get from the animal shelters. The kind that really wants to love again but just isn't sure he can trust you so you have to put treats in your hand and coax him out from behind the couch. She is able to get his hand in hers without the use of MilkBones and he timidly smiles at her. "Buddy. My name is Buddy."

So Hazel, according to the conversation I am now able to overhear in my backseat while I drive around aimlessly since no one has yet given me an actual destination, was a marriage therapist when she was alive. However, she was also pretty much addicted to having sex with married men, so her track record was not stellar. In fact, she was personally responsible for at least 20% of the divorces in Wichita Kansas during the late 70's and most of the 80's. She was killed in a hit-and-run car accident while crossing the street — ten-to-one odds that the chick behind the wheel was a former patient of hers. Looking at her in my rearview mirror with her shoulder length mousy brown hair and matching dull brown eyes set a bit too close together, along with her button nose and seemingly absent chin (her face just kind of runs down into her neck), it's actually pretty impressive. Part of me wants to turn around and say 'Well done!' and offer her a high five. But unfortunately the exchange between my two fares has wandered back to Buddy and like a marathoner on an endorphin high, he's gotten his second wind.

"The thing that really pisses me off..." he's saying now, only not angrily anymore. Now his voice is more reserved. His tone more resigned. "Is that I felt superior to her because I refused to be held down by a belief system that would allow someone like her to condemn someone like me. When she would drill into my head all the ways I could end up in Hell, I would laugh at her on the inside. But then, when she finally drove me over the edge... the day I found the letters from the State of New York and confronted her about the fact that my father had been seeking custody of me for my entire life and she had kept him from me — telling me he had died before I was born. She told me that I would never be allowed to use a woman as a vessel to breed my own filth the way he had done to her... forget the fact that she drove him away with her tirades and her insanity. She blamed me for him and him for me and hated us both... and the day that little fact came home to roost, that day I knew one of us was going to die. At first I thought I'd kill her. I mean it's not like she didn't have it coming. But then I thought, when you die you stop. There is no remorse, or suffering, or regret. I didn't want to give her that gift. If anyone was going to finally have peace and quiet it was going to be me. So I went into the bathroom and took every pill bottle my mother had, ran a bath, got a glass of fruit punch kool-aid and sat in the tub taking every single pill. Mom had about twenty different bottles of old pain medication that she had refused to take when she was in pain but she also never threw away. She also had some anti-depressants and a prescription for her diabetes. Who knows what else I took. There were probably some antibiotics and some harmless beta blockers or something in the mix... but in the end, whatever it was did the job. And it turns out she was right. She was right about everything. And I had to come here. I came here because I wasn't good enough to even earn my mother's love." He said that with a certainty that made me sad. I noticed he was not crying anymore, his hands now moving through his sandy blond hair instead of across his wet face.

Then I get angry. Why would he have to come here? Is it because of the suicide — because he would rather be dead than continue to live as the emotional punching bag for his own mother's venomous abuse? Is it because his mother wished it on him? And if so, where will she end up?

I've met more people down here in the last few days than I ever would have thought I would meet and the funny thing is a lot of them — most of them — seem like decent people. I know I've said it before but it's worth repeating. This place sucks! I'm planning to talk to Deedy about this. Not that I think he has any actual authority, but I have to talk to someone about it and he seems better at accepting my venting wrath than most.

Hazel is being endlessly patient with Buddy. She's a picture of sympathy, stroking his back while he talks on and on and smiling while she cups his face in her hands — pulling him in for a hug every once in a while. And he seems to be responding well. He's actually starting to smile. And occasionally even laugh.

Fuck me RUNNING!

What is going on in the back of my cab? "Okay kids!" I say with just a bit of panic. "It's time to end this magical ride, so I need a destination from both of you. Buddy? Where to? Hazel? You seemed to really want to get somewhere when I picked you up." Neither of them is listening. Hazel has morphed into a school girl before my very eyes.

"I was just so silly. I thought I needed to assert my independence by only making myself available to unavailable men. But I missed out on the greatest part of finding someone new," she's telling Buddy.

"What was that?" he answers.

Don't say it. Please don't say it. She's going to say it.

"The chance you'll find someone you can love." she purrs at him.

I slam on my brakes in the middle of the road, and take a tiny bit of delight when both of their heads are thrown into the back of my seat with tremendous velocity.

"Get out! Both of you! Get the fuck out of my cab!" I can't believe this is happening. I'm screwed. Falling in love? In Hell? That's got to be in the top 3 most offensive things that anyone could conceive. My job just turned into a carnival goldfish you win for pitching dimes. DEAD IN THE WATER. I'm screaming now. It's my turn to come unglued. "I mean it! Get out!!"

Buddy looks at Hazel. Hazel looks back all dreamy-eyed at Buddy. "I think we are finally getting somewhere." he says and they leave the cab together hand in hand.

As I watch them leave, I do have to admit that it seems like they are made for each other. He's got enough baggage to keep her psychologist chops sharp, and he will adore her and only her, which is far overdue in her life. It's not that I'm against love. I just don't want it happening on my watch.

"Louise?" Tim's voice comes through the radio. "I'll need you to head back to dispatch now." I can tell he's looking forward to seeing me about as much as he looks forward to root canal.

"On my way Tim"

On my way to get fired again.

I am currently sitting on a curb outside of the cab company holding my second pink slip in as many days, staring down at the words, "Terminated for Facilitating Love." How ridiculous is my life? Or my afterlife? I mean, really. Who gets fired for facilitating love? I am feeling a bit sorry for myself. But I actually feel worse for poor Tim. He looked like he was going to cry when he handed me this slip. Poor, slow, sweet Tim who I don't care what terrible or horrific thing he may or may not have done in life does not in any way shape or form belong here. And he deserves a way better day than he had today — having to fire the Hellverse's worst employee ever. But before I left he grabbed me and pulled me into a giant bear hug, patting me on the back so hard if I had anything stuck between my teeth it would have dislodged it better than flossing. Like I've said before, human touch is very rare down here so however awkward or uncomfortable that bear hug was it was also kinda cool — pretty much the coolest thing ever so far down here, almost as cool as Deedy, but not quite.

Speaking of Deedy, it is time for me to haul my sorry, leather-clad, once-again-fired ass back into his office. I'm not really sweating the whole telling him this time because I know he will be his usual understanding self and probably be more interested in hearing about the little girl and any uncovered memories than about my seeming unemployableness. That's pretty much the only thing that I'm not sweating in this ridiculous outfit. I am starting to chafe and I still have about five blocks to go to the Agency.

My mind starts to wander as I begin my long, hot, thermodynamically challenged walk. I start by thinking about Deedy's reaction to my losing yet another job, and wondering if there will be another one behind it, and I suddenly think, "It's just like my Mom and Dad — always taking me back." From out of nowhere this is what fills my head, and all of the memories that single thought brings with it.

Off and on throughout my life, one of my parents would get the bright idea that they were somehow enabling me, that my bad behavior was being reinforced by their placid acceptance. Unfortunately for them, they never got that bright idea at the same time. So, usually it would inspire a new round of "good parent vs. bad parent" in which good and bad is entirely objective and changes considering your personal perspective. Oh, and it would spark the most wretched fight nights I've ever remembered. My mom and dad were like something out of the movies most of the time. High school sweethearts, married when they were still technically teenagers, and have brought the other into every single delusion since. Dad goes on a diet and Mom starts worrying that he'll waste away. Mom takes a Thai cooking class at the community college and Dad talks about her like she's being courted by the French Culinary Institute. If Dad says the sky is green, Mom agrees. If Mom thinks that Furbees are little instruments of Satan, Dad is right on board with the idea. The closest thing to an argument that they would have under normal circumstances would be Mom's rolling eyes or Dad's criticism of a dry roast.

Enter the "non-normal circumstances," namely me. I was the only thing that could tear these two incredibly silly, stupidly-in-love people apart. There were some nights when I would lie in bed listening to them scream at each other, saying unimaginable things. It was like in those moments they totally forgot they loved one another. And the thing is, it's not because one of them loved me more than the other. It was because both of them loved me so completely that regardless of what side of the argument either of them were on at the time, they were each willing to sacrifice the feelings of the other in order to further their own cause.

Those were the worst times of my life. You would think that the most horrible way you could ever see yourself is through the eyes of someone who hates you. But you would be wrong. Because I can tell you that it is way fucking worse to see yourself through the eyes of someone who loves you, really loves you. Because that's when you have to face the truth... that some people love you in spite of who you are, not because of who you are. In the case of my parents that was abundantly clear. Even to me.

During those times I would have done anything to make them stop. Usually that meant leaving. Sneaking out in the middle of the night hoping that by the time they figured out I was gone they would have forgotten which side of the argument each of them was on and just forgive each other. Sometimes I would crash with a friend, but eventually Mom and Dad caught on and starting the next day they would call all my friends until they found the one I was staying with and convince me to come home. So I started wandering out further, staying away longer. I knew that when I was gone they would worry, but not fight. I was okay with that. I liked the idea of them having a normal life without me coming in and screwing it all up. Ultimately it would be my love for them that would drive me back — that and the need for a home-cooked meal. But primarily it was the fact that I missed them. So I would come back swearing to them and to myself that this time would be better. This time there would be no fighting because I wouldn't give them a reason to fight. I would turn things around and be a better daughter. Of course, that would last as long as it took to score some blow, or to pick up some random loser guy, or get picked up at a party by the cops. And the funny thing is, when I would get home and my parents would have that resigned looks on their faces, I'd also see something else behind it. Love — always love — my love for them and theirs for me — unconditional love. And it could have killed them, it could have destroyed their marriage, yet there it always was. It would have been so much easier if they just stopped loving me or if I could have stopped loving them, become estranged and never speak again. Over time they would have been better off for it, no matter what had happened to me. But none of us could conceive of that kind of type of love — that artificial pretend love that continued to haunt me in my adult relationships. Was it my fortune or their misfortune that I was one of those kids, born to those parents?

The long, hot walk to the agency combined with the little side stroll down memory lane did make me much more melancholy by the time I got up to the 17th floor. Gabby was waiting with a cup of glorious coffee. She handed it to me the second I got off the elevator. "Hiya Gabby. Where's Will this afternoon?"

She glided over to me and waved her hand dismissively. "He just hasn't returned from his morning assignment," she said, as though it was nothing for me to worry about.

"But his morning assignment was following me at the cab company," I said, with equal nonchalance, although mine admittedly was a bit artificial. I was actually kind of worried about the kid.

Gabby looked at me as if I'd just grown another eye smack dab in the middle of my forehead. "My goodness, you are smarter than you look Louise," she said with genuine surprise. Then she tossed back her head on that long glamorous neck of hers and laughed.

Have I mentioned that Gabby's outfit has hardly changed since I met her? She's always wearing different a dress, that much is obvious, but the general style has remained the same — the same Donna Reed vibe day after day. I've always wondered how she managed that, but I have also learned that folks that hang around the second chance temp agency rarely acknowledge let alone answer personal questions. So, I've learned to put my curiosity away when I'm here and just sit back, keep my big mouth shut, and enjoy the many perks of employment by Deedy and company. And as if she was reading my mind, (which she probably was, the little minx) Gabby handed me another fresh, steaming cup of coffee before she said, "Don't worry about Will, I'm sure he'll be back before you are out of the boss's office."

"Yeah," I responded. "And this promises to be a marathon." I sigh, heavily. "Is he in there?"

A voice comes booming from the back filled with humor. "Gabby, have you seen Louise? Because being this is my office, I would assume she would come to see me and not hang out in the lobby with the help. Wouldn't you?"

Gabby giggles — a bit girlish herself. What is it today with men turning women into giant gigglers? "Better get in there," she said.

I found myself smiling this time too, as I walked into Deedy's office and announced, like it was a major accomplishment, "I got shitcanned again." and tossed him a quarter.

Deedy was obviously amused. "My darling girl, you seem to be taking this one better than the last."

"Yeah, well, I've learned there's a lot more fucked up down here besides my employment issues. Can we talk about Tim at the cab company?" Deedy rattles the curse jar and I deposit my penance.

"So…" I say expectantly.

"We could talk for years about Timmy, but nothing that will answer any of the burning questions in your mind. Sorry, Louise. Can't be helped. Let's talk about you instead. I'm sure you've made some interesting discoveries, right?"

"No, you can't dismiss me!" I respond vehemently. "I get that I am not allowed to ask you personal questions, or Gabby or anyone around here, but there's some things that I need to understand!" Even I can't believe that I'm being this demanding. I sit up straight in my comfy chair as if I am harboring way more confidence than I'm actually feeling. I decide to also add just a bit of manners in case it would help my cause, so I end with "Please?"

Deedy's voice is calm and kind, and his eyes are soft yet penetrating as looks deep into mine. He even leans a bit over the desk and it has the desired effect. I'm frozen in his gaze. "No, Louise, you don't. The universe, whether in life or the afterlife, is filled with things you may not understand. It is not your job to know everything. It is your privilege to learn what can be learned and to experience what can be experienced. And to decide what part you are supposed to play in every situation — good or bad, glean what you can and leave the rest for someone else."

"But it just isn't fair." I say with sincere emotion. "The fact that Tim is here, or Mrs. Barnes, or Buddy, or that poor little blond girl, all of these people being down here with the scum of the former living… doesn't make sense."

Deedy laughed a little. "You know Louise Patterson, for a woman who died at age 45 and found herself damned for eternity, you have quite a misguided sense of justice."

"And that's bad isn't it," I say, pouting just a bit.

"No, in fact, it's quite refreshing." he answers. "Now, can we talk about you? So I assume you saw the little girl? Since you brought her up again?"

And so I launch in to telling him about my, yet another, strange day. I tell him about the little girl and her new companion, the incredibly handsome man. And the fact that pretty boy seemed to know an awful lot about me, and used a very unappealing nickname, yet it seemed somehow... intimate.

"Are they real or are they are figments of my imagination?" I ask.

"Why ask me? If they are figments of your imagination when only you would know — wouldn't you?" he asked.

I sigh heavily. "You are determined to be as uncooperative as possible, correct?"

Deedy looks at me with unadulterated pity. Then he smiles wide. "Have I ever told you that in Wales there is a theatre that has these words inscribed on it: Creu Gwir fel gwydr o ffwrnais awen.'"

"Those are not real words." I say.

"Yes, they are. They are Welsh words," he replies.

"Then I'll need you to translate Mr. Welsh guy!" I say exasperated.

Deedy laughs again. "It translates as 'Creating truth like glass from the furnace of inspiration'"

"How does that apply? Or is it like the sheep thing and you are just homesick?" (Yes, I am quite aware that I'm being a shitbird right now, but I'm still pouting and Deedy is being all life-lessoney.)

"What that means darling girl, is that sometimes you have to walk through fire in order to be prepared to face the truth and other times you just have to have a little inspiration. And that applies to you in so many ways," he chuckles once more as he lets his sentence drop off.

"Wait a minute. Did you just make a Hell joke?" I look at him like he is insane.

He gives me a playful wink. Then he reaches into his desk and pulls out another yellow sticky note.

"You've got to be kidding! I've got another job! Already?" I exclaim not knowing whether to be grateful or to start crying.

"Yes, but you can't have this precious sticky note until I've heard the whole story," Deedy said. "What happened today, Louise?"

"Oh!" I tell him. "Well, sit back and get ready to laugh your head off, because I have the story of at least one lifetime!" I say excitedly. Deedy reacts equally and leans back in his chair to get more comfortable. I then begin regaling him of the freak show that occurred in my cab earlier. Deedy was practically hysterical when I recounted poor Buddy and his rant about his mother. And Hazel's penchant for married men and how Buddy had just warmed her heart like the Grinch at Christmas and how they ended up walking off together like the end of a romance movie. Deedy actually had to wipe away a tear from laughing so hard.

"And how do you feel about that, Ms. True-Love-Is-A-Myth?" he asks teasingly. I can't believe how quickly I became so comfortable with this stretched out, beautifully dressed, cartoon man. I simply stick my tongue out at him as a response.

Then I told him about the walk home and the memories that were haunting me the whole way here. I told him about my mother and father, their fights, how I used to leave but I how I always came back. Deedy got very serious once more, "and why, Louise?"

"Why?" I ask.

"Yes, why do you think you remembered that at this moment?" he answers

"Because seeing Buddy and Hazel made me think about how conditional love can be. Except for those two people who always seemed to love me without regard of even themselves." I was surprised at just how profound my own answer sounded even to me.

"So, today was a good day to be Louise, because today was the day that Louise remembered 'agape,'" Deedy says matter-of-factly. "What is with you today and making up words?" I sound exasperated. Deedy laughs one more time. "Agape? It's a lovely word, and a very old one. It means unconditional love— the rarest love of all."

"Nice word." I say wistfully.

"Quite." says Deedy with sincere affection. We look at each other and smile. And my heart, however artificial or imagined it may be, also gets a little warmer today.

12

Okay, so now I'm heading back to my apartment floating on super heated air. Before I left Deedy handed me the yellow sticky note. And it's unbelievable! Tomorrow I start work as a hairdresser. Yes, I'm well aware that I have no qualifications whatsoever to be such a crazy thing, but nevertheless tomorrow that is exactly what I will be. In the spirit of full disclosure, I did tell Deedy that I have never cut hair, not even on a dog or a kid, let alone an actual grown-up who cares about how they look. Deedy's response was, "All the better!" It actually served to remind me exactly where I am and how my non-qualifications could be an asset.

I know what anyone in the world would be thinking right now. Why would anyone go to a beauty parlor in Hell? And what is it that is being cut, since hair (like every other body part) is just a fabrication created by the dead. But I would remind anyone who questions this that Hell is supposed to imitate an earthly city, just shittier. And people crave things that make them feel more like they used to, especially women. So the hair salon down here is pretty busy, surprisingly.

And I am all of the sudden very excited about the prospect. It sounds like a pretty easy gig! I mean, I have no problem making people look worse than they did when they came in. And who's ever fallen in love or planted a garden, or did anything that wasn't just narcissistic or vain in a salon. I mean, getting a haircut is not necessarily sinful, but once you're in the salon chair, thinking about how you are gonna look when a professional hair person is done with you? That, in a strictly old testament way, probably falls under vanity, otherwise we would all just be taking kitchen knives to our hair or just letting it grow out until we look like Rapunzel. So, the idea of getting a temp job that sort of punishes people for something that is sort of kind of wrong — sounds like a winner!

So, as I arrive home to my apartment, peel off the wretched leather, throw it into the paranormal closet followed by a nice view of my middle finger, and settle into bed, my mind is filled with all kinds of possibilities.

Tonight my dreams feel familiar, like an old favorite movie that you stumble upon on a rainy Sunday. I find myself stopping in the dream just to soak up and enjoy the sense of homecoming and to relish not being chased by invisible monsters.

When I was growing up in Small Town, USA it was very rare that anything out of the ordinary happened. Occasionally, some poor, unaware stranger would accidentally stumble into our little hamlet and right before he or she contemplated suicide or ran out of town screaming, they might stick around long enough to create a buzz. But that didn't happen nearly often enough. Every once in a while a local kid would get a wild hair up his ass and decide to rob a liquor store or the convenience mart. That would be amusing — watching our finest in blue chase down some wanna-be thug. And of course there was the one time when we made national news, after an octogenarian who lived on the outskirts of town (in a shack by the way — a fucking shack!) died and her house was condemned and the construction workers found $1.7 million dollars in cash under the floorboards. That one kept tongues wagging for quite some time.

Anyway, those kinds of instances are few and far between. But every single year, without fail, come mid-June, the main road into town becomes bumper-to-bumper color and light and promises of great things to come — because every year, Mid-June meant fair week.

The county fair was advertised as an exhibition of business, agriculture, the arts and sport. Businesses from all over town would literally shut down their storefronts and relocate to the fair grounds for the week at the fair. Local farmers would haul out their home grown produce and livestock to show, auction, or sell. And their wives would sharpen their claws in order to tear each other apart in various baking, canning or jellied competitions. They even had a table setting competition.

The "arts" always made me giggle when I saw it on a billboard or a brochure since it basically entailed a cutest baby photo exhibit, a birdhouse making workshop, a taxidermy competition, and a few local bands screeching out their versions of *Mustang Sally* or *Brown-Eyed Girl* for a half-dozen drunks.

But the sport? Holy shit... the sport! The sport was always the very best part of the fair. Because "the sport" meant the Rodeo. Sure, they also had a demolition derby and a bunch of fat middle-aged guys dressed in old-timey uniforms playing baseball, but no one really cared about all that. The rodeo is what put butts in the seats at the county fair. Bulls and clowns and barrels brought out the families and the old folks. And the cowboys brought out me and my pals and every other red-blooded female in a 150-mile radius.

Every year we would all show up in droves, dressed to the nines in our tightest jeans and tallest boots and spend the day at the rodeo ogling the cowboys as they smacked dust out of their jeans with their great big cowboy hats.

Then, when the sun went down it would be time to hit the midway. The midway was truly a magical place, transforming a giant empty field into a paradise filled with carnival rides and barkers claiming their game would ensure you the very biggest stuffed animal in the fair. Not to mention, funnel cakes, popcorn, candy apples and anything you could possibly want (and a few things you have never thought of) deep fried and served on a stick. Some of the best times of my life were at the county fair.

And tonight I'm back there — enveloped by the lights and sounds and smells that make me feel instantly at home and happy. I'm walking with other people, I think Linda is there and a few others who could have been strangers or friends forgotten. It's dusk and I can almost feel the breeze coming in with the darkness, as it tends to do in the world of the living. I can hear laughter ringing in my ears from every direction, and some of it belongs to me. I feel content.

Next thing I know I'm all alone. I have a faint memory of being here, in this situation, once before. This actually happened to me. I was about 33 or 34 years old at the time. Linda had already met Hank and left earlier to spend some alone time with him, and my friends Tammy and Syndie and I were walking the midway when two yahoos from a bordering town came up and started telling them all about the sheep they were showing at the grandstand the next day. Next thing I know they are walking off arm in arm with those two rednecks and I am left standing alone. Even though I realize this is a faraway memory, I can't help but feel fresh pain, as I realize I'm alone in the one place that you never want to be all by yourself...the county fair.

I make my way to a bench that is not occupied by a pregnant women or harried moms trying to wipe off a sticky faces before they attract the dirt right out of the air. Once I locate an empty bench I do what any grown ass woman whose best friends just abandoned her next to the kiddie rides at a carnival is supposed to do. I sat down and started to cry. Not sobbing, snotty crying, but weeping quietly to myself. "Fuck them." I say to myself, "if they'd rather hang out in a stinky barn filled with livestock over me." I'm just beginning my little self-pep-talk when I realize that I'm no longer alone on the bench. I look over to see a pretty young girl sitting next to me. She appears to be about 20 or so, with incredibly long blond hair that shines under the lights of the carnival. She's wearing old dirty jeans, worn out sneakers and a tee shirt, and when she speaks she has a pronounced southern accent.

"Hey. You Ok?" she says in my dream, and I realize she said it to me in life as well.

"Yes, I'll be fine. Just being silly." I say, quickly wiping away my tears.

"My name's Sue-Ann," she sticks out her hand and I take it. "I'm Louise," I respond.

"Nice to meet ya Louise," she says. Then, suddenly much shier than she was when she sat down, she begins her tale. "See Louise, I work for the Harris Shows, the rides that are here? And I have a friend who works in our office?" she formed it as a question and nods her head to a trailer that says 'Corporate Office - Harris Shows' that is sitting right across from our bench. Isn't it funny that the trailer has probably been there every year and I'd never noticed it.

"So, any ways," she continues, "my friend, well he kinda noticed you and he wanted to come over and say 'hi,' but he didn't want to upset you even more... so he figured if I came over and met you first, maybe it'd be okay if I introduced you to him?" The whole Jeopardy-answers-in-the-form-of-a-question thing is annoying, but other than that she seems very sweet. So, even though my brain is screaming, 'these people are carnies and probably trying to figure out a way to rob you blind!' I still find myself looking at her and nodding my head in consent.

She smiles a wide smile and motions over to someone behind me. "Bobby, come on over!" and she stands to make room for the stranger.

He sits down next to me and I look up and gasp. I can't tell you if my reaction in real life was the same when this event actually happened to me, but dream me has forgotten how to breathe. I'm looking into the lovely face of the man with the little girl. "Bobby?" I say. "Nice to meet you," and I stick my hand, that I'm sure is trembling, out towards him.

"Hello. And you are?" he says in the same voice I heard earlier today, in Hell.

"Louise." I answer

"Well Louise, do you not like my carnival?" he asks teasingly.

"I love the carnival. Is it really yours?" I ask.

"Well, kind of. I'm the manager of Harris Shows, so for now it is my carnival. And I hate to see pretty girls cry at my carnival." He looks at me and smiles and I feel the warm glow that his smile brought to my nightmare the night before.

"I'm just being a huge baby because my friends ditched me for farm animals." I say laughing. "Don't take it personally."

We look at each other and grin. I see the night ahead of me, in this lucid dream that has become a memory. A memory locked away inside of a broken, dead brain that has been less and less reliable as my expiration date got closer and closer.

I suddenly remember that we spent all night that night together at the carnival. Like two teenagers on a first date, we walked hand in hand, got cotton candy and rode every ride. We joked like old friends and when we stopped in front of a milk bottle game and I talked the barker into giving me an extra ball to win a big stuffed tiger, Bobby looked down at me through those lenses with those deep blue eyes and said, "I think I might have to start calling you 'Weasel' instead of Louise." I mockingly punch him in the arm and say, "That does not make me sound very attractive at all." He stops and takes off those glasses and looks deep into my eyes. Before I know it, he is kissing me. Not a lecherous, cop-a-feel kind of kiss — a real kiss, a first kiss, a kiss that says 'Get used to this, because I'm planning to do it a whole lot more.' And then he wraps his arms around me and I start to cry again, only this time not because I've been forgotten. This time because I've been found. I am home here, in these arms — protected, soothed and loved.

I wake up and it takes a minute to remember that I am dead. I am dead and Bobby is alive and we were a couple once. I know this to be true deep inside my damned soul, even though past that night I still can't remember. But, I know that I loved him and he loved me. How did I forget that? How did I forget that I had not just a lover, or even a boyfriend, but a real grown-up, loving relationship? I have to talk to Deedy. I must tell him that I identified the man from the street and from my previous dream — Bobby, otherwise known as Robert James Callow, in management for one of the largest amusement companies in the world. He traveled five months out of every year, yet the rest of the time he was mine. MINE! I spring out of bed with a sense of both panic and renewed excitement. So Bobby is not a figment of my imagination but a ghost of a memory that has manifested down here. That has got to mean something, right? All these memories, bizarre dreams, everything that is happening to me since the moment I found that notice tacked on the bulletin board at the coffee shop means something. I am changing. Maybe my future is changing too.

And the little girl — must be Linda! I was closer to her than anyone else other than Bobby. It's all so clear now! She's manifesting as a child to remind me that we were the queens of embracing our inner children! The eternal bratty kids who downright refused to grow up — never took anything or anyone seriously. Now, even though I'm stuck down here, I have to find a way to make this work. I can hardly wait for today to end so that I can go see Deedy and tell him all about this new revelation. I can almost see his face. Big, huge, grin just for me!

But first, I have to pretend to know what I'm doing as a hairdresser. This should be fun, and this may be the job that I get to keep longer than a day. I feel it in my construct of a skeletal system. When I take a peek in the closet I am both surprised and more than a little pleased with what I see. Granted, I'm not going to be walking any runways at fashion week in Paris anytime soon with this outfit, but it's really not hideous either. A pair of old lady style shorts, the kind with an elastic waist band (for extra comfort!) and that fall just above the knees. The top is of course some unnatural fabric that promises to fit terribly and is the color of cat puke, but still, over all, not bad! Once I pull on the shorts I realize they are at least 2 sizes too big. The elastic holds them up but creates a balloon effect so that I look like a giant pear shaped pile of cat puke. So why am I grinning from ear to ear? Because other than the orange jumpsuit — this is the best outfit I've ever gotten from that "loves-to-fuck-you-up-the-ass-every-single-day" closet and that, along with my brand, spankin' new memory of Beautiful Bobby and Me, just goes to confirm it.

Everything is going to be different — starting today!

The walk to the salon is short, which is good considering what I'm wearing. Not because of discomfort, but because of the looks I'm getting from my fellow Hellions. Remember how competitive we are down here when it comes to our closets? Yeah, well today's outfit might just get me cut up, so I'm more than a little relieved when I see the salon sitting before me just 2 blocks from my apartment. I glance across the street at the coffee shop where I found the original notice for the agency. I stop for just a moment and get a little nostalgic. It seems so long ago since I reached out and took that note of destiny, although in terms of real time it's only been a few days. But I feel like I've lived a lifetime in these limited hours. I reach up and brush away just the hint of a tear. 'There's no time to cry now, ya big baby!' I say to myself. 'It's time to make a few others cry!' and I stride into the salon.

The second I walk in I feel at home. I am going to assume that the short, portly woman standing in the middle of the room cussing everyone out is the owner. My eyes go wide with combined surprise and admiration as I watch this diminutive woman put everyone in their prospective places. She's wearing a housecoat, probably not intended for use outside of the home for the living, but for us it's all fair game. It's a very bright yellow with a huge print that suggests something has been spilled all over it, but the changing colors that are depicted say 'no, somebody did this on purpose and called it fashionable'. On her feet are a pair of lime green high tops a couple sizes too small, so she's cut out the toes and let her piggies free. I think I may have found a mentor down here. I say this because as all these thoughts and observations are occurring to me, I have also heard her drop the f-bomb at least seven times. And when she says it, the word sounds like "fook", because she has a very pronounced British accent — kind of like Deedie's only she sounds more like the Queen — well, The Queen if she hung out on the docks, but nevertheless.

"You must be Louise, right?" she finally gets to me within her tirade. "You ready to get to work?"

"Yes M'am," I say, respectfully. I do not want to be on the other end of one of this woman's fits.

"Who the fuck are you calling M'am?" she says. "Do I look like the fuckin' Queen to you?" This makes me laugh out loud since I was just thinking about the Queen. But suddenly I remember that this woman's disposition is probably not going to improve if I just burst into laughter every time she says anything to me so I stifle any more.

"I'm sorry. I just didn't catch your name?" Yes, I realize that I've become a bit sycophantic, but what can I say? This broad is kinda scary.

"Name's Lottie and as of right now, I'm your worst nightmare." She sticks out her hand and I take it while trying not to laugh again. I'm guessing this will not be my worst nightmare, no matter what she may think. 'Really?' I think to myself. 'Come take a walk through my brain some night.'

"So Lottie," I start, trying to convey a friendly and conversational demeanor to her. "Are all these people here for a haircut?"

Her voice suddenly became docile and almost polite. "Well, this gentleman would like to hear the lunch specials and that woman over there is here for a kidney transplant." Obviously Lottie is a master of sarcasm. Then the old Lottie came back with a vengeance. "Of course they are all here for foockin haircuts! Blimey, what did Deedy send me this time? A fookin mental?"

Okay, so maybe she is scary, but I also think I just might be a teensy bit in love with her. Not in a lesbian way, more like a 'this is who I want to be when I grow up' way.

"Come here newbie, and I'll show you how we make fookin magic." she says with a guffaw-type laugh. "Welcome to the most fun you'll ever have in Hell, cookie!"

I rush over as she escorts an older woman into the hot seat. I feel excited as the woman says "Just about a half inch off. That's all." and Lottie looks at me and gives me a wink. I start to get excited. I actually start bouncing on the balls of my feet like a child waiting to see what's behind some visiting relative's back. She began her lesson with "The first thing you do is listen carefully to the customer." Then she grabs an enormous pair of shears and lops off a huge chunk of this woman's hair from the back. "Then you do the exact opposite!"

I was born for this. I can do this job for eternity. And eternity is exactly how long I've got. I immediately turn to everyone waiting and say "First victim, step right up!"

The next 8 hours fly by. People keep coming in. I don't understand why. I mean, really... we've already collectively asked why they initially come in. But then not only do they come in to groom something that doesn't really exist; they sit there and watch us butcher every single person's hair before them. It's like those breathers that drive super slow by a car accident because they can't resist seeing the carnage and possibly a body part or something else really gross. But the part that astounds me is that still, after everything, they get up and get into my chair and every single one of them tell me, sometimes beg me, not to do to them what I did to everyone else even though a part of them has to know that that is exactly what I'm going to do. People left my chair in tears, or screaming at the top of their lungs. One guy actually took a swing at me! What a day!

Of course once they get back to their domiciles and sleep, 90% of them will wake up looking the same as they did the day they arrived, which might be why they come in. Their curiosity and sense of boredom outweighs the risk of being scarred forever.

And the best part is that it is practically the end of the day and I have not screwed up! I do a little dance as I sweep hair off the floor. It's going to be officially named heretofore my 'I made it through a day of work without getting shitcanned' dance. Lottie also has decided that she thinks I'm the shit, so we are chatting and laughing and having a generally surprising good time considering where we are in the big picture when the bell on the door rings. "Looks like one more for the day. You up to it, newbie?" says Lottie. "Of course!" I answer right away. "I'm a natural!" Lottie laughs low and soft. "Yeah, I think you just might be." she agrees.

I look up to see who will be next in my chair. Standing in front of me is a frail girl, who looks like she may be in her early 20s. Her face was stunningly beautiful even without make up. I could describe how thin, yet still curvy and feminine she was, how striking her gray eyes were, how she seemed to be dressed tights, bike shorts, and a puffy shirt all in contrasting colors. But no one walking down the street or running into her would have noticed any of that. All they would see is her hair. Her hair was awful, and keep in mind I've been giving people bad haircuts deliberately all day. This was worse than anything I had done in the last 8 hours. "You poor thing." I say breathlessly. "You seem to have already gotten a haircut today!"

She looks at me at gives me the most emptiest of smiles. "Yeah." she said in a childlike voice. "I did this to myself. I do this every day, and every morning I wake up and it's back. Can you help me?" When she said the last part it was almost pleading. This girl doesn't need help with her hair. She just needs help.

I sit her in my chair and put the smock around her shoulders, squeezing them as I do. "So tell me..." I say and sit in the chair next to hers "why would you do this to yourself?"

"I'm here aren't I? Not here in the shop. I mean *here* here. I'm obviously not a good person. I may as well look as bad on the outside as I seem to be on the inside." She looks so sad, I once again find myself wondering about this crazy place and how so many of us ended up here. I stand behind her and run my fingers through the mess that is her hair. While I do that I say, "You want to tell me about it?" And for a minute I feel like Deedy, making someone come to terms with their own damned soul. That thought makes me a smile.

And so she starts talking, and while she talks I'm snipping away at her hair like I've been doing this all my life. Stopping occasionally to look her in the eye from behind her in the mirror and offer an, "Uh Huh" or "Yes, I know." so that she'll continue.

She tells me about how beauty was her obsession in life. So much so that she was unable to function sometimes. She dabbled in drugs, but not to get high — usually to stay thin or because she needed to stay awake to exercise more. She spent all of her disposable income and a lot of other people's too, on the latest laser treatment, or botox, or some kind spa. She always had perfect hair, perfect teeth, and perfect nails. And whenever anything started to fall she'd be in her plastic surgeon's office getting it picked up or made bigger, or smaller, or tighter. At the end she didn't even recognize herself in the mirror anymore. And no one else did either. She talked about how boyfriends would leave her when they couldn't take her constant need for validation any longer. How all of her friends thought she was becoming unhealthy and so they would drift away. She died alone, leaving a corpse that was more silicone than actual body parts. She made a joke about not needing to be embalmed because there was nothing organic left and I forced a laugh. Then she woke up here and found that she had not brought any enhancement with her. She was at point zero. She looks younger then she was when she died because she was so young when she started trying to re-engineer her looks.

I look at her with amazement. "This was you before you did anything?" I say incredulously.

"Yes." she says sadly, as if I'm looking at the most wretched thing ever placed on earth.

I turned her chair around and made her face me. "You realize you are absolutely beautiful. I would kill to look like you! And I'm a person that others describe as self-assured... to say the least." I'm continuing to snip at her hair as I talk. "From what you have told me, you believe it was your vanity that brought you here, and so now you are trying to pay penance by trying to erase any signs of your ego at all. What if you still haven't gotten it right?" I stand back and look at my handy work. I have actually managed to fix most of the damage. And I'm not a real hairdresser! However, her gorgeous face is now framed in a cute bob. I start to brush it out to make it shine as she asks me her one question.

"So, how am I supposed to get it right?" she looks at me with hope in her eyes. I know what this means, but my heart begins to ache with the need to provide her with something to hang onto down here. So I finish brushing out her hair, I whip her chair around so that she can see her reflection, and I say "Understand that you've been beautiful the whole time."

Tears well up in her eyes as she runs her fingers through her now perfectly cut hair. I can't help but feel just a tiny bit proud of myself. Then she stands and gives me a long, tight hug. "I may not be able to do it today. But knowing that someone out here thinks I'm pretty is already enough for now." I squeeze her back and just enjoy the human contact for a moment. Then as she leaves the shop I collapse into my chair. At least, it will be my chair for five or ten more minutes until Lottie gets a hold of me. I cringe at the thought of that. But suddenly I look up and Lottie is staring at me with complete wonder.

"What have you done, luv?" she asked quietly.

"I've apparently lost another job," I say back, and smile at her through my tears.

I'm slouching in Deedy's comfy chair like a sullen teenager. And Deedy is looking at me from behind his desk with a bemused expression, as usual. That whole boyish charm thing that made me feel so welcome when I first got here is starting to get on my nerves. After about five minutes of nothing but that smile since I told him all about the girl in the shop, I just look at him and roll my eyes. To which he responds by leaping forward in his chair and placing his chin on his folded hands and says "I think there is an American expression Louise, so you've probably heard of it. Something about practicing what you preach?"

"Here's another American expression," I retort, "Shut up!"

Deedy laughs. "Now no need to be temperamental darling girl."

"Apparently not," I say with an almost smug tone. "because, from what I've been able to gather about The Second Chance Temp Agency, it's not about the jobs but about my uncanny ability to lose them."

"That's almost profound." he says and again adopts his Deedy-is-so-amused face.

"I've made another observation, while we are having this discussion. Every time I have come in here there's not been a single other client. Are there more people that come here or is just me? Deedy adopts his infomercial voice and says "The Second Chance Temp Agency has helped hundreds of thousands of people just like you find their true purpose in the afterlife."

Then back to the same old Deedy. "However, darling girl, Your insistence that the universe — to include the Hellverse — revolves solely around you is always an amusement for me."

I just look at him. "Whatever." I say with a bit of disappointment. "I was beginning to think that maybe you were my Hell equivalent to a guardian angel — if there is such a thing?" I pose the last part as a question, just in case he's willing to answer it.

"Let's not speculate." Of course he's not going to answer it. "Let's stick to the facts. You told me about the poor dear in the salon and how she felt when she left. But you forgot to mention how all of it made you feel, Louise." He sets his chin down on his desk, actually resting on his desk, and looks at me expectantly.

"Well, I felt as good as anyone who's just been handed a termination slip can, I guess," I say with a smile, because I know that termination slip says that I was fired due to "Recognizing Beauty." I point at that on the slip and ask Deedy, "How could anyone feel really bad about getting shown the door when it's for something like that?"

Deedy looks at me with feigned confusion and shrugs his shoulders. One more time I find myself laughing in Hell. Deedy is laughing with me.

"Then on the way over here I had another memory..." I started, and Deedy pushed himself up with keen interest. So I continue my story.

When Linda got married, everyone knows how badly I behaved at the rehearsal dinner, but before that when all getting married meant to either of us was an excuse to shop for pretty dresses, Linda and I were in our glory. We had a blast going from store to store trying on all the clothes, drinking complimentary champagne, standing on those pedestals with the mirrors around them feeling like princess fairies, and basically avoiding any real conversation about the great event that all of this was leading up to. We stopped into a small, local bridal boutique early on in the process — a small shop owned by an elderly woman everyone called Miss Shanie. Miss Shanie was so excited that we were there that she immediately began rushing around the store grabbing dresses for us both to try on — beautiful wedding dresses for Linda and, well, interesting bridesmaid dresses for me. Now, let me say this right off the bat. I had no intention of buying my bridesmaid dress from Ms Shanie. She was a sweet old lady to be sure, but the accent on that has to be on the word old, especially when it came to her taste in auxiliary wedding fashion. While her bridal gowns were traditional yet stunning, her bridesmaid dresses were awful. A few of them I swear were made of the exact fabric of my grandmother's throw pillows in her "fancy" living room where no one was allowed to sit — ever. You literally had to avert your eyes and try not to take the entire thing in at once with most of them. Ever been to Vegas? Walk into any casino and look down at the carpet. I heard once that casinos notoriously pick out the ugliest carpet patterns so that you'll avert your gaze and keep your eyes at slot machine level to make you more likely to stop and gamble. Bridesmaid dresses used to have the same basic end game. To be so hideous that everyone at the wedding would look only at the bride at all times.

Linda and I planned to look at a couple of wedding dresses for her and then leave with a polite excuse and head to the outlets in the next town. But Ms Shanie had different ideas. She brought out a pink-ish nightmare on a hanger and showed it to me with the same giddy enthusiasm that a young child has when presenting a handful of crushed dandelions to his mother claiming it's a bouquet of beautiful flowers. The dress was so horrific that Linda and I just looked at each other and immediately fell out into peals of laughter. However, the reaction that was apparent on Ms Shanie's face prompted me to straighten up and make a half-hearted excuse about too much champagne, which of course, prompted Ms Shanie to suggest that I try it on. So I took it from her, holding it like a cobra about to strike at my face, and made my way to the dressing room.

Now, you know how sometimes when you see something that looks really bad on the rack, but once it's on you and you step back and really look at it, you realize it's not so bad? That didn't happen to me. The dress fused to my body like a bad science fiction movie monster. There was so much fabric I could never be really sure that my arms were in the actual arm holes and there was some sort of flower-slash-bow thing that was pinned to the chest but was so big it covered part of my face. And, regardless of how many yards of unnecessary pepto-bismal pink satin was killed to make this dress, it still had a mermaid skirt. So I couldn't walk more than three inches a stride. When I exited the dressing room I was met by Linda laughing so hard I kept waiting for her to pee herself. Ms Shanie on the other hand regarded me with great concern and kept circling me and making these "tsk tsk" noises until finally she stopped and said one word — one word that destroyed me and Linda for the rest of the day — "backwards." We started rolling with uncontrolled laughter. Even after I managed to get out of that wretched straightjacket of a dress and we had somehow made it out of the store without reducing Ms. Shanie to tears, we were clinging to each other as we stumbled down the street trying to catch our breath from laughing so hard.

"That was a deeply traumatizing experience." I say when we were finally able to speak.

"I may never be able to scrub that image off of my brain." Linda says in between gasps. "Now I know what everyone means by some things can't be unseen!" she says giggling once more. We continued to laugh and hold each other like children as we walked down the street to the bus stop.

In the next town, we came across the glitzy dress shop where all the private high school girls bought their prom dresses and the like. Inside there we both spotted a little lavender dress that promised to accentuate my assets in an amazing way. As I stepped out of the dressing room, now being embraced by the softest silk fitting my every curve, other customers actually stopped their shopping to gaze admiringly my way. Linda looked at me with glazed eyes and said "You are going to be the prettiest girl at my wedding!" with total enthusiasm and pride.

But that statement bothered me, for whatever reason. While normally I seek out those kinds of compliments, in this case I felt, and still feel, that there was something severely wrong with the idea of a bride who does not believe that she herself is not the prettiest girl at her own wedding, which is why I ended up doing the single craziest thing I'd ever done up to that point in my life. Unless you haven't been paying any attention whatsoever to my tale up to this point, that covers a shit load of crazy.

The morning of Linda's wedding I woke up to a screaming brain cursing me for a night filled with brown liquor and toxic words directed at my best friend. With that fateful (and regrettable) rehearsal dinner toast still playing a highlight reel inside my head, I found myself in front of Ms. Shanie. And to her delight I handed over a couple hundred dollars for the ugliest bridesmaid dress in the universe and then I actually wore it to Linda's wedding.

To be sure when Linda first caught sight of me in all my hideousness the thought crossed her mind that I was trying to mount a final protest. But once she realized that it wasn't anything like that, and that my intentions were actually kind of noble, she grabbed on to me and held me close for a very long time. During that embrace we finally got an opportunity to thank each other for the years of friendship, for every great experience, forgive each other for every transgression and express our total devotion to each other all without saying a single word.

Deedy sits back in his chair as I finish my story and looks at me with gentle affection. Finally he says "My Darling Girl, I must say you, are always a pleasant surprise."

"Speaking of surprises!" I had almost forgotten my epiphany from the night before. I excitedly begin to relay last night's dream and it's revelations.

"So, Bobby is someone special?" Deedy says while scribbling as if he's taking notes in my file. I have long suspected however, that he just doodles.

"Uh Huh," I say excited once more. "I can't remember how long we were together or whether it ended badly, but I do know that we were very much together and very fond of one another. I cannot believe that I had forgotten him actually. Is it weird that I did?" My words are just pouring out. I don't really expect an answer. But Deedy looks at me with a kind of sadness and replies "No, down here all kinds of things are lost."

Now it's my turn to sit back in my chair and regard Deedy with anticipation. "And I figured out who the little girl is!" I say. He regards me with mild suspicion. "And the little girl is?" he asks.

"Linda!" I announce, then launch into my whole 'inner child' theory, complete with every psychological term I've ever learned or read to explain why she's appearing to me as a cute kid instead of as herself.

Deedy looks almost preoccupied. He says, almost to himself, "Fy merch annwyl, eich bod mor agos."

"You are speaking Welsh again," I say, bringing him back.

"Sorry," Deedy says, seemingly shaking something off then moving forward with his usual gusto. "You are very close now Louise. Tell me, how does that inner child you speak of feel about coming out to play?" he asks.

"Why?" Now I'm suspicious.

Deedy slides yet another sticky note across the desk. Yay! Another temp job, and apparently this one is going to be fun!

I jump up and grab it from the desk, looking down at it for my new gig and the air around me constricts like hands wrapping around my throat. I suddenly feel wobbly and sink back down in my chair before I fall over. I feel my blood, as imaginary as it may be, sinking down to my feet. For the first time ever in Hell, I feel chilled to the bone. I struggle to find the word 'no' inside of my head, but it gets lost in the horror of the word in front of me so instead I let out a scream.

The sound of my own scream clears the way for my mouth to start forming words. "I...I...I...no," is the best I can do.

"What did you just say to me Louise?" Deedy rises from his chair and leans on his desk. There is no more concern for me. He is as stern as he's ever been. I look into his eyes and realize that they've suddenly become hardened. I feel like I'm in the principal's office getting in trouble. I realize that I've never felt this way in Deedy's office before.

"I can't do it Deedy. I can't!" I'm not firm or definitive. I'm pleading with him. My chest feels like it weighs a thousand pounds and the tears have started again. Damn tears, this time hot with panic and fear.

"Yes you can. And in fact, you will." Deedy has calmed a bit, seems nice again. Yet, he's obviously done asking. He is officially telling me what to do.

Well, I can dig in my heels too, buddy! "Maybe you think I can. But I won't!" I say, with new tears streaming down my face.

But Deedy doesn't dig his heels in, he just sits back down behind his desk and states his case in a remarkable way. "Louise, I have never faulted you for ripping out of here with a sense of confidence. Well, let's be honest, with a sense of *over-confidence* in each and every job I've handed over to you. Nor have I ever held it against you when you came back again and again feeling defeated or like a failure. In fact, I've actually encouraged you to seek out the positives in every one of these attempts, despite the futility of the job itself. And finally, my darling girl, I do not and never would fault you for being afraid. Show trepidation, question me as to why I send you somewhere, sit and wallow for a minute or two if you must in your own fear of things that have not happened yet. But then go, Louise. Go where I ask you to, because if you deny me, as heartbreaking it would be for both of us, it would signify the end of our relationship for now and the end of your relationship with the agency permanently. Do you understand?"

I am now openly sobbing. My fear is wrestling with my sense of duty to this incredible man who has offered me so many chances, all of which I've come up wanting. I nod my head at him. Of course, I will go, not because I think I deserve this punishment, and it is a punishment to be sent to such a wretched place. Even though it scares me shitless, I will go because Deedy is asking me to, and he is right.

I look at Deedy now with a pleading and pitiable look and say through my still flowing tears "Will it be dangerous?"

"Perhaps." he answers frankly. "But that's where you have to trust that I would never send you somewhere hopeless. Follow my directions and you will come out fine."

"Then that's enough for me." I say with a trembling voice that does not portray any of the assuredness my statement tries to convey.

"Go home darling girl and get some sleep. Tomorrow everything will seem brighter," Deedy says with a sense of finality that actually rouses me out of my chair.

But out in sweltering heat of the streets of Hell I cannot imagine that is true. In reality, I cannot imagine anything regarding tomorrow. Every time my thoughts turn to tomorrow and the events that will or may occur I have to stop and shove them out before I start screaming in the street.

Because tomorrow, I start the hardest job ever — the one job I would have thought would always be saved for someone so much worse than I — a job only the truly damned could do.

Tomorrow I start at a Day Care Center.

Tonight sleep is an escape fraught with images, all very disjointed, yet pleasant. None seem to gel into a story. It's like a montage of all my favorite things and faces — mom leaning over my bed with her eyes full of love as I am dying; dad throwing his head back in laughter; Bobby smiling at me and grabbing my hand; Linda and I driving down the highway singing at the top of our lungs to the radio; a bouncing red ball against the sidewalk; the feel of rain on my face. You would not believe how much you miss rain in Hell.

Suddenly my alarm goes off. It feels sooner than it usually does — entirely too soon. I'm not ready for this day to begin. I have a small argument with myself. What if I just don't go? Really? Are you ready to say goodbye to Deedy and any chance of redemption? C'mon Lou. Just get up and face it. The sooner the day starts, the sooner it ends and hopefully it ends with a termination slip. Just go, do something fabulous, and wait to get fired.

In the meantime, I have to wrap my head around these children. These demonesque creatures, the scariest of the scary in the entire Hellverse becoming my charges. The thought of it drives me into my small bathroom retching with dread and terror. I emerge a few minutes later trying to wipe the taste of bile out of my mouth. I make my way over to the closet and open it without the same apprehension that normally goes with it. Today, I have bigger fish to fear. But as soon as I open the door I burst into laughter. This is the true genius of the closet in Hell, to make me laugh on the single most terrifying morning of my entire afterlife. For hanging in said closet is my bridesmaid dress — the dress I told Deedy about yesterday. Is that a coincidence or is it more? I don't know, but I am actually comfortable with the familiarity of it, and of course with the memories it brings fresh to my battle-worn mind. I close my eyes and imagine Linda standing in front of me and with tears in her eyes she looks at me and says, "Thank you for this."

I look at her with my mind's eye and say out loud, "Thank you for everything."

As I start my walk to the address on the sticky note, I'm totally unaware of the others around me. My legs are getting heavier and my gait is lumbered and slow. I am thinking I may be sick again when I see the center looming just ahead. Looking around I realize that other than the center, the street is empty. No other business, no homes. But of course, who would want to live next to this? Even in Hell it is probably important to keep these demons out of the general population as much as possible. However, it does seem like a bit of a kindness to the rest of us, considering where we are. We are all Hellions. None of us have a different future than any of these poor small creatures. So, out of logical thought or perhaps avoidance of my immediate future, I also ponder my own fate. Why am I here, standing on an empty street in the boondocks of Hell? Why am I being punished so harshly? Was it that over-confidence Deedy spoke of? Is this the end of the line when you are fired from every other temp job or are the sins of my life to be paid for in death? But if I've learned anything about anything in Deedy's little job corps, it is that my life was filled with some good too. Why make me remember the good if this is my only option — to play babysitter for horror personified?

This makes me angry, which is good, because that is what I finally need to drive me through the front door and enter the day care center. As I swing open the door I catch a reflection in the shiny glass that takes my breath away and makes me feel a bit faint. Will, attempting to be clandestine is about a half a block behind me. He really is terrible at the whole hiding thing. But I'm so glad that he's here! First, it means that Deedy isn't so mad at me to throw me out here without any protection and second it may be the only friendly face I get to see here today. It's with that small comfort that I enter the center.

It is incredibly quiet inside. Like, this is what folks mean when they say 'It was too quiet'. I had never really understood that phrase before. Primarily due to the fact that I abhor quiet and will do anything (talk to myself, put Buffy reruns on a loop) to never have to abide it. Now, would it be better if the place was filled with howling or screaming or the sounds of torture? I don't know. But this is fucking unbearable. It feels like any noise that I may make will just evaporate before it even hits the atmosphere — like I'm in space.

I was just about to give it the old college try and start shouting out when suddenly my ears and my mind are filled with a cacophony of noise. I cannot tell how many voices are growling, yelling, or squealing at once but it's so overwhelming that I put my hands over my ears to block it. Then, suddenly, the silence is back. Only now it's accompanied by an older black woman standing in front of me. She looks just a few years older than me, maybe 50. Her hair is disheveled and her clothes more so. There are some tears in the fabric and I see some stains that I hope against hope are not blood on her shirt. Her shirt is man-sized but styled straight from baby gap. It's bright orange with a lime green flower on the front. In the plus column, it looks comfortable.

She looks at me and says, "Louise?" I respond affirmatively and she must have sensed my next question by my face because she answers before I ask. "Oh, we have the little monsters behind the strongest, thickest, most soundproof substance in the Hellverse. It saves everyone else from the torment. Unfortunately, it does nothing for you. I'd offer you earplugs, but, well, look where we are. None are available." She gives me a weary smile.

"That's okay. Is it going to make a bad impression if I say that I just want to get this day over with?" I ask.

"Nope. Welcome to Child Care in Hell," she sticks out her hand and I take it. "I'm Dani. Nice to know you."

She takes me back and we stand in front of the heavy doors. "Once they open, you have to get in before anything gets out. So no dilly dallying. And make sure they know who's boss right away or else you'll get creamed. And try not to look them in the eye. The eyes are old, even though the body is young. It can be a little disconcerting. Remember these kids were once the most influential, albeit most evil adults on earth. Watch out for flying objects and never ever turn your back on any of them. We try to do everything here on a buddy system, and I'll be your buddy today, so I will try and cover you and I'd appreciate it if you do the same. However, if things get real in there, then it may be every man for himself for a minute. Got it?" she recites all this like I'm heading into a war zone. I feel a new prick of fear up my spine as I realize that I probably am heading into just that.

I take a deep breath, swallow a few times to make sure I'm not going to puke again, and steady myself. "Okay, I think I'm ready," I say in a voice that sounds about half as unsure as I actually feel.

"Then come on in," she says. "Oh, and by the way, nice dress," she says with a laugh. I laugh too, until the door opens.

I jump in quickly as instructed and see a frenzy of big and little people running around. Mainly, the big people are chasing after the little people, although there is some evidence that occasionally the big people are running away from the little ones. There are toys, but mainly soft toys. There's nothing in here that could be fashioned into a weapon. Unless you count the guy in corner with his juice box aimed like a machine gun and spraying everyone who comes near him with red liquid. 'Good' I think to myself, 'That's what was on Dani's shirt, not blood.' I realize that I've just taken my first breath since I entered this room.

The room itself looks quite typical. Like any other day care center — brightly colored carpeting and small tables and chairs. There are giant crayon-colored totes filled with stuffed animals and quilted wall hangings featuring happy children at play or letters of the alphabet. In the corner there's a play kitchen with a plastic stove and refrigerator filled with plastic food. There are some things that are conspicuously missing, like games with small pieces or any game that creates a sense of competition. These kids probably take the whole 'doesn't play well with others' thing to an art form. There are also no army men or anything that resembles a weapon. I don't know if that is to keep them from getting any ideas or to stave off any memories of life. But it's probably a good idea. There also are no outdoor toys such as trikes or toy cars, most likely because these kids are rarely let out of the boundaries of these walls.

While it's loud and crazed and a bit like the "before" footage on one of those nanny programs on television, I feel a bit of relief. I think I can handle this. There's no ritual sacrifice or other illicit activity as far as I can see. I take a few more deep breaths and begin to get my bearings. I see a bookshelf in the corner. I go and sit in one of the only chairs they have, which are chairs made for children. So with my knees practically touching my chin I begin to peruse the titles of the books. They are all quite virtuous, and they are geared toward older readers than the age of the average child here. But considering that these kids have brains much more advanced, it makes sense. I look over the titles and see one that is dear to me. "Little Women" by Louisa May Alcott. I remember the summer between sixth and seventh grade when I broke my leg and couldn't go outside and play. That summer promised to be a bereft season filled with loneliness until I met Jo and Beth and Amy and Meg. And of course Laurie, the young trust fund boy who lived next door and each girl, to include me, kind of fell of love with him during the course of the story. I can do this, I think to myself. I can share this wonderful story with these poor demented children and show them how self-sacrifice and helping one another can bring great reward. That should accomplish two things, it might make it a bit quiet and more manageable in here for a while, and it just might get me fired! So, with great gusto I announce as loud as I can, "Story Time! Anyone who wants to hear a lovely tale, come sit down!" Three or four children immediately come and plop down in front of me with faces full of expectation.

'Hey' I think, 'This is easier than I thought!' Now I'm dreaming about

Deedy's face when he hears that it turns out that this, the one job where I had no confidence, is the one where I excel. I open up the book and start to read "Chapter One, Playing Pilgrims..."

Dani comes over and says "Are you okay, because I have a situation in the nap room that I have to handle."

"Sure" I answer, "I've got this!" My mood is now practically soaring. I go back to the book and start this lovely tale of Christmas in the March household, with beloved Marmee and her girls. I barely even hear Dani as she says "Okay, but don't let this get out of hand, only three or four kids at a time okay?" I brush off her comment and continue to read. She thinks I'm still afraid, or unsure. She doesn't realize that I'm in my element.

A few minutes into the book more children wander over. I see them in my peripheral vision, looking at one another before taking a seat in what I'm now calling 'the story circle.' I've read this book so many times the words are coming easily and I am able to get lost for a few moments in my own thoughts while I continue. Who knew? All these kids need is a little structure, something to get lost in and look forward to! Now I am in an even grander fantasy. I am going to be the hero of the day care center! Everyone will be so grateful that I came here and gave them a few minutes of peace and quiet. Dani will write a letter of recommendation for my redemption telling everyone at the Second Chance Temp Agency that I revolutionized how they approach their kids now. They might even put up a plaque or something to give other employees motivation! I see Deedy standing there with pride on his face as I stand in front of the new symbol of Child Care Excellence that hangs on the wall. I can't wait to tell him he was right. That he finally sent me to the right spot.

I see the more children coming over and sitting down. Some of them are standing just outside the circle listening but haven't yet committed. I feel a wave of pride. I am sitting here surrounded by Hell children listening to me read.

Surrounded by Hell children.

Surrounded.

Damn, Damn, Damn it all!

Suddenly I remember where I am. These are not normal children. These are the demonic souls of serial killers, dictators, tyrants, and psychopaths. I look around quickly for back up. Dani is nowhere to be found. What did she say? She had a situation. I remember that. Fuck! That's why she said no more than three or four kids at a time. Why don't I listen when other people tell me things? I get lost in my own ego and think they are underestimating me instead of trying to help, which of course was what they are almost always doing. The other adults that are employed here are all around the room with their "buddies" doing exactly what they should do, paying attention to their own sets of devil charges, and to each other. No one has noticed that I've gotten myself into a shitstorm of trouble.

I start to rise out of my chair. "Okay, break time." I say with overt cheerfulness. But there's no escaping now. They have formed a strategic circle and three of them are standing guard while the rest descend on me. Fear wraps around my heart as little hands wrap around my body. I hear a growl in my left ear and turn to face it. I find myself looking into a pair of wretched, horrific eyes. His gaze seizes mine and holds me just as each child finds purchase on my dress or body and pulls me down. I feel the scream starting in my abdomen and by the time it reaches my throat, so does he. His little hands wrapped around my neck and his pale blue eyes are filled with hatred, but also longing. He wants to strangle me to death. But I am already dead. I feel his frustration in my gut. So he will do the next best thing and inflict as much pain on me as possible. They are all standing around me, cheering him on and holding me down. My head is spinning with the words 'why' and 'no.' But that is all I can manage. My brain is reverting to its most primal urge — to survive. I'm prying at him and slapping at the dozens of hands and knees now all over me. I feel a stab of pain in my legs. One of them has bit me — now another on my arm and another on my shoulder. I begin to sob as I keep trying to fight them off. There is a ringing in my ears but underneath I think I hear Dani yelling, "get her out of there!" I thank Dani mentally but all that is escaping my throat now is a ragged kind of wail, like a cat who caterwauls before he dies. The room is getting dark, but in the gray behind my many attackers I see her — the little girl with the bouncy ball. What is she doing here? Why would she come into this horrible place! Can anyone else see her?

"Linda!" I say and she looks at me. There doesn't seem to be any reaction to the fact that I am under attack. She just looks at me as if to say

"What?" My cognizant mind is slipping. Perhaps I'm hallucinating, but I can't risk her really being here. "You have to get out of here," I say, barely whispering my words, yet she seems to be able to hear me just fine.

"Stop helping!" she answers in her usual petulant way. "But I have to. That's my job." I say now, barely conscious.

"What job!" she says to me teasingly.

"The most important job ever," I say, not even sure that I'm speaking aloud anymore. "My Darling Girl, the job of being your Mommy."

And everything goes black.

13

I am sitting with Mom and Dad in the living room watching yet another episode of 'Wheel of Fortune' when the phone rings. I leap over the back of the sofa, run to it and stand over it breathlessly to see the number on the caller id. Mom says something about me acting like a teenager and I stick my tongue out at her to prove her point. I look at my Dad and say, "I'm actually a little nervous."

Dad says, "why buy a vowel? It's obviously, 'You can take it to the bank.' you moron!" Then he turns his attention to me. "Just jump right in front of the bullet baby. That's the best way." That's all I'm going to get, because now he's yelling at the next contestant for guessing, 'You *can make* it to the bank'.

I pick up the phone and say, "Right on time! So how much do you miss me?"

Bobby's low raspy laugh is the only response and even after four years together, the sound still makes my thighs ache. "I miss you more than I miss Elvis!" His standard answer, for which I wish rolling my eyes made a noise so he could hear it. Bobby loves Elvis — like total-pathetic-fanboy kind of love. Because of all the traveling he does, he has learned to live with very few material possessions. I drag him into clothing stores hoping this time he will agree to a few more shirts, or a new pair of jeans. But no, he will gladly sacrifice any sense of fashion and at least a third of precious suitcase real estate for his miniature Elvis shrine. I always make horrible fun of him for it, but in reality it is just one of those quirks that make him different from anyone else — one of those things that made him able to convince me to fall in love with him after years of self-induced exile in the world of romance.

"So what's new in the world of amusements?" I ask breathlessly, indicating to anyone with any powers of deduction that I am just being polite because I have something way more important to impart. But no, he settles in and starts to tell me about three new rides with all the features and ticket sales and whatever else that under ordinary circumstances puts me to sleep. Then he says, "Oh, and Sue Ann is in love with a local again," sarcasm dripping from every syllable.

Now, I love Sue Ann stories. Sue Ann, bless her, is more hormonally challenged than I ever was. She "falls in love" at least twice a month. Her heartfelt romances usually end with her climbing out of the back of a pickup truck and swearing to keep in touch while throwing his number away in the nearest trash can. I adore Sue Ann. But today, even the promise of a few vicarious thrills from the girl that took me out of the game by introducing me to my dream guy is not enough to keep me quiet.

"Well, I have some big news!" I say. My mom comes rushing out of the kitchen to stand next to me and I silently wave her off. Privacy in this house can be a commodity sometimes. She doesn't move, so I say, as quietly as I can, "can I tell him on my own please?"

"Is that Mom?" he asks. I love how he calls my parents Mom and Dad. They love it too.

"Yes. She's excited." Suddenly I know how to spring the news. "You see, because you are far away, I had to tell Grandma and Grandpa first." Then I wait.

"Grandpa and Grandma? I thought your grandparents were dead!" He can be truly clueless, but in an adorable way.

"They are." I answer.

Then it hits him. "Weez!! Really? Are you sure?" he asks quickly.

"Yup. Got professional confirmation this morning. You are not going to believe how many doctor's appointments this is going to require. I may need to go back on drugs after this." I say laughingly.

"We are going to cure you of your White Coat Syndrome yet!" he says, obviously excited. "Is there any risk in the pregnancy?" he asks with sudden concern.

"Dude, I've been clean for almost 5 years!" I say, assuming he meant due to my drug history.

"No, I mean because you're so...." he trails off.

"So... what?" I ask accusingly.

"So... OLD!" he yells into the phone laughing hysterically.

"Fuck you very much!" I say back. He loves to tease me, simply because I am five years older than he is. Stupid Jerk.

However, having brought that up, I do have to admit that having a baby at the age of 38 was never in my life plan. "The doctor says there's always some risk with women my age, but since I'm relatively healthy, he isn't worried." I say proudly, as if I had total control of the condition of my body.

"Baby, you are a testament to clean living!" Bobby says with affection, and yes... more teasing.

"Have I said 'Fuck You' today?" I say back laughing right along with him.

"I love you Weasel" he says, and I know he means it.

"I love you too." I answer, and so do I.

I feel like a virgin on prom night. I am truly that nervous and self-conscious, which is ridiculous. Bobby is coming home as he's done a hundred times before and he will hold me and kiss me and tell me how glad he is to be home where he belongs. I'm not sure if I am nesting or if this is due to the fact that Bobby missed the entire first trimester, as well as part of the second. I'm terrified how he will react when he sees me in my hugeness. Linda keeps telling me to get a hold of myself and that I sound like a neurotic wife. Linda is a bitch.

Bobby and I are not married. First of all, I abhor the idea of institutionalized commitment. He doesn't agree but he loves me enough to be somewhat compliant. That is the other thing that is bugging me. Since he successfully got one past the goalie and knocked me up he has brought up the idea of marriage more often. But I don't think it's real to him yet. It's still a concept of me being pregnant. Once he sees me in all my glory, I'm half afraid he'll knock me over the head and drag me to the altar by my hair.

Anyway, our house is closed up at least seven months out of the year. Bobby travels, and can only come home for occasional weekends and our fair week, and I hate living alone, so I move back in with Mom and Dad when he's gone. Every fall, when there is a chill in the air and I realize that carnival season is coming to an end, I return and open up the house. But this time I'm running around like a chicken with my head cut off. Linda is hanging out, supposedly to help but mainly just to put flame on my anxiety fire. I've dusted at least twice, the windows are wide open so the crisp autumn air can drive out the musty smell, and I'm vacuuming. I look at Linda who took the slipcover from off the sofa, sat down and turned on the television and has now clocked at least three hours in front of it. "Hey! Pregnant girl doing tons of manual labor over here!" I say.

"Studies have shown that exercise is good during pregnancy. So are you going to relent and name your kid after me or what?" she responds.

This is the argument Linda and I have had ever since I found out I was having a baby. What to name it. If it's a boy, of course it will be called Bobby. However, if it's a girl... well, that is still up for debate. Linda wants it named after her. Bobby wants it named Marie, after my Mom, and I want it named Willow after a character on Buffy the Vampire Slayer. No one is compromising at this point.

"Is that what this is? Blackmail?" I ask accusingly. She laughs out loud.

I look at the clock and realize we only have 20 more minutes before Bobby is due back. I run and put store bought cookie dough in the oven. I heard once that real estate agents do that when they have open houses because it makes people feel at home when they smell something baking. Linda comments that Bobby will think he's in someone else's home. So I do the only thing left to do to make my house presentable for the man I love.

I kick Linda out.

Now I'm in front of the TV, lost in an episode of Friends when I hear Bobby's key turn. I instinctively stand and grab a throw pillow from the sofa to hold in front of me. The first thing I see when he walks in are those gorgeous blue eyes. They still leave me breathless. You know how people say "Absence makes the heart grow fonder?" Well, I hit the jackpot in that regard. Because every single time he walks in the door I get to fall in love with him all over again.

He walks up to me and snatches the pillow away. Then he looks at me as though he's ogling a 22 year old supermodel in a bikini. By the time those baby blues get back up to meet my gaze they are filled with love and desire. "Damn Weez. You look amazing!" He leans over and kisses me deeply.

I wrap my arms around his neck and reply "Who knew you were a chubby chaser?" and then I wrap my legs around him and we fall onto the sofa. His kiss is passionate yet his touch tender. He has always been a generous lover, but this time he is mind-blowing, better than ever. I'm gasping for air and riding my third climax in less than a half an hour when suddenly we both sit up. The fire alarm is going off.

Damn real estate agents.

14

I'm in the hospital. Eating lime jello and staring at the most incredible miracle I've ever laid eyes on — my darling girl. She has Bobby's eyes and just a wisp of white blond hair. All she's done so far, besides being born, is cry and sleep. Yet, I find her fascinating. I just want to watch everything she does every minute for the rest of my life. She is only a couple hours old and she already has made at least seventeen different expressions on her tiny face. I am thinking that she is going to be very smart. The nurses come by every few minutes to press on me and check my vitals and encourage me to sleep. But who could possibly sleep after having such an amazing experience? Well, Bobby apparently. He's snoring on a chaise lounge next to me. But I have just let go of the only person with whom I ever shared that much of myself for that long. For almost a year she went everywhere I went, she ate everything I ate, she was part of me. Now she's outside, in the world, and I will never be able to get that close to her again. Except for feedings, she and I will never be connected again. All of a sudden I find myself crying. My heart is full, my life is happy.

Bobby wakes up and crawls in next to me in my hospital bed. He stares at her for a few minutes and then looks at me. He wipes the tears from my cheeks and says "Why is it that all the greatest moments in my life involve you weeping?" I smile up at him.

"Okay, we have to do it." I say

"Do what?" he replies

"Pick out a name." I say

"We can call her Willow, if you insist." he says kindly.

"Actually, I was thinking she looks like a Linda," I say and begin to cry all over again.

Welcome to the world Linda Marie Patterson.

My Darling Girl.

We are at the Easter Egg Hunt at Mom and Dad's church. My darling girl, who we now call Dinny to tell her apart from Aunt Linda, looks adorable in that pansy blue dress that Mom just had to get her. She's running around looking desperately for eggs but having no luck. I tried to be her spotter but she gave me the whole pouting, "stop helping!" thing so I'm on the sidelines trying to will her toward the obvious colored orbs lying within two feet of her.

Bobby comes up and wraps his arms around me. He's been so good lately, coming back for holidays and giving whole weeks to his assistant so he can come home more often. I put my hands over his and lay back against his chest. I love the feeling of being wrapped up in him. Even now, after almost ten years we are still like brand new lovers. He still hasn't managed to get a ring on my finger, but in every other way I belong to him totally.

"Hiya Baby Daddy," I greet him warmly.

"The girl having any luck?" he asks

"Nope, assuming you're talking Easter egg hunting. Now if you're actually referring to retaining her most-precocious-kindergartner-ever title, I think she's got it in the bag!" I reply.

"We did make a great kid didn't we?" he says

"Yup. In fact, I've been thinking. I don't think I can bear another letter to Santa asking for a baby brother or sister for Christmas. Perhaps we should think about making that happen for her?" I ask. And yes, I too have a hard time believing I was volunteering for childbirth a second time, just in case anyone was wondering.

"We'll talk about it after your doctor's appointment." he says matter of factly.

"Seriously? I really don't think it's anything to worry about!" I protest.

"Weasel, I honestly don't care what you think, unless you have been secretly going to medical school. What I do know is you would be willing to ignore something serious if it meant avoiding a doctor's appointment. Now I love you and I always will but it's time to let go of this fear and take things seriously. I'll be leaving on Tuesday, but your Mom promised me she would take you to the doctor this week and I expect a full report." He seems so determined.

"I kinda dig it when you go all 'Me Tarzan You Jane' on me," I say. "Fine. I will go to the Doctor and we'll find out that it's just a fibrous cyst or something. Then we can get back to talk of making babies." I sound so much more confident than I actually am. The lump Bobby found a few nights ago seems to move from my breast to my heart and to my throat. Every time I think about it my stomach turns. Every time I think about the needles the Doctor is going to poke me with in order to see what it is also makes me feel a bit queasy. But I will go and endure whatever torture they have for me. For Dinny and for Bobby. For my family.

I'm back in the hospital. More lime green jello, and more nurses poking and pressing on me. Now though there is no baby to look at with wonder. I have recently endured a double mastectomy only to find out that it was in vain. My cancer has spread and is now incurable. This trip to the hospital will be my last. Honestly, I have not made peace with that yet. I don't know if that is what is keeping me alive or if it's just my family sitting around willing me to live another day. I do know that I am tired, and I feel like shit warmed over and I am pissed off beyond all reason. Linda is sitting with me now, while Bobby takes Dinny to school and Mom and Dad are home getting some rest.

"I remember when I told Bobby I was pregnant with Dinny," I start, "he asked about the risk because I seemed so old to be having a baby. Doesn't it seem funny now? That seems like such a long time ago, and today I feel so much older. But he made a smartass comment about my being a testament to clean living." I look at Linda, who gazes back at me with sad eyes.

"Not clean living, perhaps. But you were always charmed Lou. You could fall into a pile of shit and come up with an ice cream cone." she says with a quiet laugh.

"Yeah, what flavor ice cream is cancer?" I say bitterly.

"Don't start feeling sorry for yourself now." Linda chides. "When we were young you swore you wouldn't make it to thirty. The fact you have survived to forty-five means that you have been on borrowed time for a while now. And look at what you accomplished in that fifteen years."

"That's the problem, Linda. I have accomplished nothing. I got knocked up, and now I won't even be able to see my darling girl become a teenager let alone an adult. I have never had a job, or a husband, or done anything worthwhile. I have used everyone who has ever loved me. I was terrible to you and to my parents. Now I'm going to die. I will never be able to make it up to all of you." My tears are coming fast now. "I am so sorry."

"No, I am sorry." Linda says grabbing my hand, her tears coming on strong to pace with mine. "I feel so bad that you think your life means that weak description of failures. Your life means so much more to Bobby, and Dinny, and your Mom and Dad. And your life means everything to me. You're life and my life are so interconnected. I can't imagine what the world is going to look like without you. And it makes me scared to think that someday I may wake up to a life that can't be shared with you. Does that sound like a failure?" her voice is almost pleading.

"I think that means there is one thing I have always been great at," I say gently, grabbing her hand with both of mine. "I've always been good at picking wonderful best friends."

When my family returns, they all surround me — Linda, Hank, Dinny, Bobby, Mom and Dad, along with Rev. Dawson and a couple of hospice nurses. Rev. Dawson prays, the nurses attend, and. we all cry and hug and say our goodbyes. Bobby leans over and looks into my eyes one more time, "I love you so much, my beautiful little Weasel." Dinny climbs into my bed and says "Why is everyone crying Mommy?"

"Because I have to go away, and you guys won't see me anymore," I answer, my heart breaking as I do.

"Daddy told me. He said you can't help it," she responds. "And that you'll miss us as much as we miss you." Her beautiful face looking up at me with a sense of understanding even though she can't possibly grasp what is about to happen.

"Every day, I will be looking down at you." I say to her, knowing deep inside that I am lying. "And every day I will say the same thing. I hope you are happier today than you were yesterday. And I hope all your tomorrows are wonderful!" I bury my face into her hair and breathe deep, taking in her scent and trying to imprint every cell of her onto my dying heart.

Mom leans over and kisses me on the cheek. "You have always been a wonderful daughter." she says through her own tears.

"Mom, now is not the time to start practicing hyperbole," I say, laughing.

"I know I've never been good at being good." I squeeze her hand before letting go and giving out a long sigh. I look at this lovely woman.

"Promise me you'll help Bobby with Dinny."

"Of course, you don't even have to ask!" she answers.

"You were a great mom to me. I know you'll be a great mom to her. Please don't let her forget me. Just don't tell her that I was a bad person. Lie to her for me please."

"I will never tell your daughter a lie, and she will know every day how wonderful you are," she says smiling down at me.

I feel like I am finally going to sleep after a long, hard day. Only this time I am not going to wake up. As I look into the faces of the people that not only shared my life but *were* my life, I can only think of one thing to say to each and every one of them. So I say it over and over until everything fades away.

"I'm sorry....I'm sorry....I'm sorry"

As my surroundings begin to disappear, Mom leans over me once more and starts to speak. I cannot hear her anymore. There is just a rushing sound in my head that drowns out everything else. But I finally know what she was trying to tell me.

YOU ARE FORGIVEN.

15

My eyelids feel heavy. I can hear a lot of noise around me — people talking about me like I'm not here.

"I think she is coming around."

"Gabby, I found another bite. Can you heal this?"

"Why was she left alone?"

My eyes finally open and I can see Will and Gabby and Dani standing over me.

"Welcome Back Louise!" says Gabby with her usual cheerfulness.

I look at her and say "Deedy."

Will helps me sit up. "You need to get your land legs back, Louise."

"Stop it!" I say, angrily. "I will be fine, but I need Deedy, and I need him NOW. So if anyone here really wants to help me, get me to Deedy!"

Suddenly Deedy is striding up behind Gabby. He comes into the lobby, and I realize that is the first time I've ever seen him outside his office. "Bring her in, people. I get the feeling Ms. Patterson has a lot to talk about."

Will and Dani take each arm and assist me in getting up. It's amazing how sore an imaginary body can feel. I also get very dizzy once I am on my feet. Dani holds me steady and looks at me with sorrow, "sorry, Louise. I shouldn't have left you alone."

"It's okay. I guess it had to be done," I say.

"If you only realized how much that is true," she says with a faraway look in her eyes.

When we enter Deedy's office he motions to a chair. They sit me down and Deedy dismisses them with a wave of his long fingers. They leave quickly and I am alone with the man that sent me into the tiny arms of my attackers.

"So, let's talk," Deedy says. His smile and his eyes are exuding kindness and complete benevolence.

"I should be pissed at you for sending me there," I say quietly.

"People have hated me for much less," he states.

"But I think I get it now, and I understand why I was supposed to go," I answer.

"So that means, you are not mad at me?" he asks.

"I didn't say that. I just understand. And I remembered everything."

"What did you remember?" he asks

"My darling girl," I say to him. "Something you have known all along."

He just leans his chin on his hands and doesn't respond.

"My mother told me I was forgiven." I say to him, almost with accusation.

"Another thing I've known all along." he responds.

"I think I was a decent Mom, but I couldn't have been," I say, with new fresh tears welling up in my eyes.

"Why would you say that?" he asks

"How could I have forgotten her? I left her behind. I promised her on my deathbed that I would think of her every day and I didn't even remember who she was!"

"So, we are back to this." Deedy says as he opens up my file.

"Back to what?" I ask him heatedly.

"Do you want to know why you didn't remember Dinny or Bobby? Or any of the later part of your life, Louise? Here it is, plain and simple. You packed for this journey and all you brought was guilt and despair. You very meticulously took out all the good in your life before your death, and even at the last moment instead of declaring love, you made your last words to the people who loved you an apology for your life. Do you understand how much that breaks my heart?"

I look at Deedy through big, wet eyes, "breaks your heart?"

"Yes, because you are my darling girl. You always have been. You are flawed Louise. You are smart and funny. You are rebellious and a little lazy, especially when it comes to living up to your own potential. You are good-hearted and generous and indiscriminate with your kindness. You recognize beauty in everyday things and people. You are imaginative and a bit of a manipulator. You know how to love, and be loved. You are also selfish and arrogant and foul-mouthed. You make mistakes and you learn from them and you constantly move, striving to be bigger than your own little life. You are amazing. You are human. You are the fragile, yet incredibly strong example of perfection, just as I imagined you at the beginning of time." Deedy moves from behind his desk and stands directly in front of me. Not too close to touch, but closer than I've ever been to him. Then he says six words that fill my head and heart like rainwater in a barrel.

"You are exactly as I created you, Louise."

I look up at him. In those amazing eyes.

My Mr. Deedy.

My creator.

God himself.

So if you could ask God any question, what would it be? This is mine...

"Then why did you send me to Hell?"

Deedy laughs softly. "Don't you get it? I didn't send you to Hell, Louise. You did. You wrapped yourself up in every sin you ever committed and held onto the shame even when it created overwhelming heat all around you. Even when it put a cover over your eyes so that all you could see around you was clouded or hazy. You cannot even seek me anymore because every time you look up, you choose to be blinded. You could not shake it off even as you began to remember and those memories brought you some comfort, you still couldn't bring yourself to let go of the bad to let the good in. Your own memories wanted you so desperately that they started to haunt you. Begging you to be remembered, cherished, and enjoyed. Yet every day you chose to be blinded by your own guilt." He gives me a sad smile. "I am not your jailor, Louise. I am your advocate. Here to take you home."

"So everyone in Hell is there because they choose to be?" I ask, remembering those demon children. That makes me shudder once again.

"Yes." Deedy starts, "Some have to be here for a very long time before they can even start on the path that you have almost completed. Others were part of a bigger plan and they need to understand that role before they can seek redemption. Those souls that attacked you so brutally, they are the ones who lived their lives in direct opposition to creation—the angels of destruction that have to be there to make room for more achievement. Yet they punish themselves more than any other, seeking out a way to start over. That's why they not only come to Hell, but they come as children. And now they are fulfilling a new purpose, like forcing you to remember who you really are. And believe it or not Louise, even they will eventually make their way back to me."

"So, you just help each of us, a soul at a time, remember you?" I ask with awe.

"There is no shepherd that will leave a single sheep behind." he says smiling.

"Thank you." I say, with true and deep gratitude. "Thank you for finding me."

As Deedy makes his way back behind his desk I suddenly realize that I have an audience with the Alpha and Omega. So I say, "Can I ask you some questions about life and stuff?"

He throws his head back and laughs out loud. "Nope." he says, "But I'm glad to see you are back to your old self. Looks like you can handle this," and he pushes a sticky note across the desk.

"Another job?" I look at him incredulously.

"Just one more," he says.

With just a cursory glance at the note I see initials pop off the page and I look at Deedy with a steely stare. "Really? IP&FW?"

"Follow the instructions on the note, Louise. And I hope to see you soon."

And I am dismissed from the Second Chance Temp Agency for the last time.

There is no going back to my cramped apartment for a fit full night's sleep filled with dreams and haunting images. There will never be another horrific outfit come out of my supernatural closet. Speaking of, as I walk out into the street I notice two things. One, my dress has been replaced with a very comfortable night shirt. That must have happened when I was unconscious but I didn't really have time to process it what with the whole discovering that my boss was actually God and I am a Mom and other wondrous revelations like that.

Secondly, while I am still very much in Hell, noting the buildings and the other folks I am sharing the street with, the temperature has cooled quite a bit. It feels like spring outside. Not too hot, not too cold. And like there is something new in the air. I suddenly realize that something new is me, and my eternity. I was forgiven before I died by everyone but myself. Today I realized how precious forgiveness is, especially when you bestow it to yourself.

I'm heading down a very familiar block toward IP&FW, feeling like skipping or dancing but holding it together and walking. No need to attract more attention than is necessary. I pass by Mrs. Barnes' house and look in her side yard. There she is with a watering can watering the most beautiful garden I've ever seen.

"Mrs Barnes! How good to see you again!" I yell out to her. "Louise? So glad to see you!" she answers warmly. "Or to be more correct, so glad you can see me!"

"See you?" I ask.

"Well dear, you have walked by here at least a dozen times since the day we met. I've called out to you and tried to get your attention. But you always walk on by. I figured you would see me at some point," she says kindly.

"Well, today has been a day of discoveries, so I'm glad you and your beautiful garden were among them," I say. And I mean it. I am so happy that she is not in Hell as we know it. She is in her own little version of paradise surrounded by beautiful flowers.

"Well, I like to help Deedy when I can," she says. "Hopefully your assistance with creating this lovely garden helped bring about one or two of those discoveries?"

"Very much. Thank you," I say and lean over to fence to give her a peck on the cheek. She returns my token of affection by kneeling and picking a single Cala lily. "Here, Louise. My favorite flower, for you."

I take the flower and say my goodbyes. Wow, so Deedy has secret helpers who choose to live down here in order to facilitate his bringing souls home. I can breathe a sigh of relief knowing that George is probably one too. But Bad Santa? Ugh... Probably not.

I turn a corner and am instantly confronted with my old employer, IP&FW. I re-read the instructions on the sticky note and put it away. I end up taking it out again and reading it one more time. I think I've got it.

So, I stand directly in front of the entrance and turn around so that the building is at my back. Then I look across the street to the building over there. It seems so tall and big that the entire IP&FW building is reflected on the front of it. Then I walk across and into the door reflected by IP&FW. See why it took three times to make sure I had it right? I am walking into a reflection of a door!

I walk into a brightly lit lobby and cool air hits me in the face. Cool air! Everything is white on white. There are marble walls with sparkly bits that shimmer under recessed lighting. The tables and desks are made of glass. Likewise there is a huge sign over the reception area that says WF&PI made of crystal. I stop to wonder about that. There is a huge and incredibly soft carpet that is pure white with a pale blue border the color of our lost sky. The border keeps the room grounded — otherwise everything would seem to be floating. Even now it feels like sitting on a cloud. Is this Heaven? Maybe I've finally made it. People are walking around with smiles on their faces and wearing normal clothes. They stop and talk and hug and laugh. It has been such a long time since I've seen this kind of communal, well, Joy. This place is awesome! Suddenly I hear a familiar voice walking through the lobby yelling "Louise Patterson! Louise Patterson!" I look up and see Will eyeing me with a wide grin and back in his monkey suit.

"Will!" I say and run up and hug him. I hold him tight for a minute just relishing in human contact. "So, is this what you do? Just jump from building to building being the elevator man when you aren't stalking me all over Hell?" I question.

"Actually," he starts while pushing the button on the elevator and guiding me into it, "I go wherever you go. Or at least I did. I think this is my last assignment as Louise Patterson's guardian angel." He says playfully and hits the 150th floor button.

"Are you really my Guardian Angel?" I ask and then it registers where we are headed. "Holy shit! That is majorly high up isn't it?" I feel a familiar panic. Has it really been just a few days since the first time I went to the agency and had this same reaction over 37 floors?

"Yes, and I remember that you turned out to be fine. Suck it up Lou," he says with total familiarity and affection. "And yes, I was your guardian angel. And I feel I should tell you that you were my first," he said.

"Explains your lack of covert surveillance skills," I say teasingly, my grin getting wider and wider. "And you realize that means that you will remember me above all for eternity."

"I imagine that is very true," he says. "Here we are. Are you ready Louise?"

"Absolutely" and I step off the elevator into my new eternity.

The first person I see is Gabby. Well, I say person. But Gabby has wings. "Gabby! You've grown wings!" She laughs her tinkling laugh and approaches me. "Louise, I've always had wings. You just never saw them until now."

"Like Mrs. Barnes and her garden," I deduce.

"Yep. Like an awful lot of things around you. There is so much for you to see now. But for right now, I'd like to welcome you to WF&PI, which stands for Watching Family and Positively Influence. Are you ready to check in on your loved ones on earth?"

I just stare at her. Gaping like a fish out of water. "I get to look in on my family?" I say with a voice that is trembling.

"Of course you do Louise. Follow me." She floats ahead of me. 'So that's why she floats! She was flying with her pretty wings the whole time and I couldn't see it,' I think to myself.

I look at Will who is walking next to me. "So why don't you have wings?" I ask

"Not every angel has wings. You have to be an Archangel to get a wing span like Gabrielle's."

"Gabrielle? I've always thought it was Gabriel." I say with surprise.

"Yeah, well, am I allowed to tell her?" he asks Gabby.

"Go ahead," she says with a smile.

"Okay, see there's a bunch of literature out there that claims to know about us and about the boss. Of course, there are a precious few, whose names I will not mention, that profess to be the literal word of God. But while every single one of them were placed there by us or divinely inspired by us, well, we had to allow for a little misinformation. You know, otherwise there would be no point in faith," he explains.

"So every text has some truth? Every religion is a little right? Isn't that kinda messed up? I mean we've had wars and inquisitions and burning times over different religions, different points of view of over God and who he is — with each one thinking they are all right and everyone else is all wrong!" I say, with a touch of aggression.

"Again, what is faith? You guys are still learning about what faith is. It used to be using magic and knowing that the seasons will change and the crops will grow because of it. Then it was all about wandering in the desert and knowing that if you are willing to sacrifice an animal then God will be pleased. Or knowing which of a hundred names to use for God is the correct on for a certain request. Now for a lot of you it's about going to church and singing hymns and tithing. Someday you will get to the point where you realize that each and every one of you is a single piece of a giant puzzle and if you truly want to hear the voice of God, all you have to do is be quiet and listen to your own soul," Will recites that as if from rote memorization.

"Very good Will," says Gabby. "You'll be an excellent angel." Then she turns to me. "Enough questions, Louise. Now it's time for you to enjoy your redemption. See anyone familiar?" She moves out of my line of sight and I squeal like a child.

"Daddy!" I say and run up to him. I touch him and he's real! He's really here. "Baby Girl!" He holds me and I'm transported back to every great memory I have of me and my father. I sink my face into his chest and try to fuse with him. "I love you so much, Dad," I say.

"I love you too sweetie," he answers.

"Oh! This means you're dead!" I say, looking at him with sorrow.

"Of course it does. But don't worry. I had a long and wonderful life. The only disappointing thing was getting here and finding out that you were stuck in Hell. They explained everything to me and told me that I would get to see you eventually. So I've been waiting patiently for you, hoping you would remember how great you are and come find me. When Gabby called and said you'd be here today all I could think was, thank God you made it for today of all days!"

"Today of all days? What happens today?" I ask.

"Come see," he says with anticipation in his voice. We go into a small private room. Still white on white with a huge sofa that looks like you could sink into it and get lost in its comfort. We sat down and a huge computer screen appears on the wall in front of us. It looks like something from a futuristic movie. Kind of holographic but still projected on the wall. We are looking inside Rev. Dawson's church from above. There is a crowd gathering inside. Some of them are people I know, I remember. Others are strangers.

Speaking of crowds, this room is getting crowded too. I look up and more and more people are entering. My grandparents, who passed away when I was young, I look at them and wave. They wave back. There are others whom I don't recognize and Will who comes by and sits on the arm of the sofa next to me. I look up and him and grin.

"There are no words for how I feel right now," I say to him.

"Just watch and enjoy." says Will patting me on the shoulder.

There are now voices coming from the computer screen and I instantly zero in on one. It's the voice of my Mom. She's talking to a beautiful woman dressed as a bride. Mom looks old. But other than that she is my mother and once again salty tears start to flow. "I miss you Mom," I say to myself.

"You look absolutely gorgeous Dinny," Mom says. Dinny! That woman is my daughter!

"Grandma. My name is Linda. I'm 34 years old, now. Don't you think I am a little too old to be called Dinny?" she rolls her eyes and I laugh. She only looks like me when she's making sarcastic faces. Other than that she is the perfect morph of me and Bobby. "She turned out to be a looker and a half!" I say proudly. "Like mother like daughter," says Dad next to me. "And wait until she gets outside the church and you hear the mouth on that girl. The acorn did not fall far from the tree," he smiles down on me.

Mom's eyes well up with tears. "You'll always be my Dinny, and I'm proud of you. I know your Grandfather would have loved to have seen you today. He would have told you that you look like your mom."

"See how well she knows me?" Dad says proudly. "And he would have loved to dance at your wedding," Mom says, now bursting into fresh tears.

Dad leans over to me and says, "Don't you puke on me bitch!" and starts laughing uproariously.

"Speaking of mouths, Dad! Jeez!" I proclaim. "Watch your language! You are in like, the holiest of holy or something!" I look at him as if I'm appalled.

"Eh, it's worth a quarter. It's a great gag!" he says dismissively.

Back on the screen, Mom and Dinny have been joined by Linda. Seeing her makes my heart lurch. "How did she do after I died?" I ask Dad.

"She was inconsolable for a while. But life moved on for everyone. She became very close with Dinny. When she and Hank lost their home during the recession of 2012, they got an apartment in the same building as Dinny and kept an eye on her. She still visits your grave regularly, and changes out flower arrangements depending on the season. She was a good friend to you."

Linda and Hank have had hard times, but have weathered them together. That makes me feel good. Then I ask, "And Bobby?"

"Bobby should be showing up any minute now to walk his daughter down the aisle," dad says. "Be prepared, he will be with his wife. He married a woman from work, about five years after you'd gone. Name of Sue Ann? She claimed to have known you and she made a beautiful toast to you at her wedding."

I just start to laugh and laugh. Good for Bobby. "Bobby always liked his women fast and loose," I say through my laughter.

And so it went on and on – seeing family and friends both inside the room and on the screen. I watched my darling girl walk up the aisle and marry. I secretly send her my best intentions and hopes for a long and happy life. When I saw Bobby again my heart began to race. He has aged gracefully, and he still has those eyes that make my stomach go all wiggly. I smile as I look down at Sue Ann. And I know what some of you may be thinking. But I know that Bobby was faithful to me when I was alive. I was burned by relationships many times before him, but he was the genuine article.

As she walks back down the aisle, hand in hand with her new groom, Dinny emerges outside of the church and looks up. "Hope you can see this Mommy," she says, seemingly directly to me. She continues, "I hope you are happier today then you were yesterday, and I hope all your tomorrows will be wonderful!" Then she blows a kiss toward the sky and I reach out as if to catch it. My darling girl, who's all grown up now. How much of her life I missed, but now I can keep my promise and look down on her. My heart feels like it's going to burst with utter joy.

Suddenly the air changes in the room. The mood turns solemn and the screen disappears. Everyone is whispering nervously and standing and straightening their clothes. I look at my Dad who is now standing straight backed like he's at attention in the military. "What's up?" I say to him, rising out of my seat.

"The Big Guy is here." Dad says, with a touch of nerves seeping into his voice.

"Deedy?" I say just as he bursts through the door.

"Deedy!" I confirm with gusto.

"Louise!" Deedy responds grinning at me. "Did you enjoy your daughter's wedding?"

"It was amazing. Thank you so much." I say to him again.

"Well, if you can handle it, I've got one more thing for you to see. Follow me, my darling girl!" and he spins and marches out of the room.

As I follow him I hear my Dad as he speaks to his parents. "That's our Louise!" he says proudly, "Twenty seven years in Hell and still she's on a first name basis with the most high Deity!"

We are walking into the common room and I look at Deedy. "I get it! Deedy... Deity!" I say with wonder.

"Rydych yn ffycin wych" he says in Welsh. "Wanna know what that means?"

"Probably not, " I answer, laughing.

"Well, now that you're in Heaven, you can always Google it." he says, smiling.

"So we have actual Internet here?" I say.

"Well, with one heck of a firewall we do!" he states.

"Can't have people sending emails to the breathers or anything." His mischievous smile makes me laugh. "Here we are, time to take a look at your new home!" He points me toward the window.

I look out and see nothing but the usual bright nothingness, and I feel the blindness coming. "It's not working!" I whine to Deedy.

"Sorry, I forgot. It is finally time for this." And as he speaks, he reaches out and wraps his arms around me. I am in the embrace of God, which fills me up and makes me feel whole, and safe, and incredibly happy. My eyes begin to clear. I look out the window again and see a wondrous world. Not apart from Hell, for both worlds exist within the same place. There are whole neighborhoods that to me looked like empty parking lots. There are mountains in the distance with great mansions on them, and I see the tops of the buildings, many with people and a few with angels actually on the roof enjoying the day or having parties. There are angels in the sky too, and overlooking the city. There are parks, playgrounds, pools and dog parks filled with happy people and animals. "All of this was here the whole time, and I never knew it." I say.

"You once was blind... as the old song goes," Deedy says with a smile. "Now you have to choose a new place to live, and a new job. Wait until you see the real estate choices you've got now! Full Amenities! And, the best news is here you can be anything you've ever wanted to be, whether it is a chocolate taster, fashion designer or an encyclopedia salesman!" He looks at me expectantly.

"Okay," I say thoughtfully, "But I thought I had a job. Working as a temp for you?" I look at him with my request glowing in my eyes. I don't want to leave the agency. And if there's nothing more for them to do for me there, then there has to be something I can do for others. He meets my gaze and smiles wide. "I was hoping you would say that!" he answers.

I am standing in a chain store in the corner. It's weird being invisible to some people. When I walk down the streets now they look so much cleaner and brighter than they used to, the hazy orange-ness that I used to think was emanating from the heat was actually coming from me, keeping me blind. Now that my eyes are open, I know the streets are filled with loving, happy people. There are always conversations, reunions, and hugs and kisses. People like to enjoy the always-temperate weather by gathering outside, sometimes for a feast or to dance. But the lost ones go by without ever seeing us. Like Martha, the woman I have to deliver this sticky note to. She's folding thin, threadbare towels for a display inside the store. Tears are cutting little rivers into her thick, overdone make-up. Her dress looks terribly uncomfortable, with its hard, rough material that is red and white. I'm pretty sure it might be an actual circus tent.

I take the sticky note that says:

DO YOU BELONG HERE?
CALL US TO FIND OUT!
SECOND CHANCE TEMP AGENCY
(666)-573-2236

And stick it to the next towel she will grab, then I stand back and watch while she finds it and looks around then places it inside her bra. I giggle, knowing she won't hear me as my mind reaches back and I remember when I found mine. It is hard to believe that was me — angry, hard, wallowing in my decimated self-image. I kind of envy her for the experiences she's about to have. Remembering is different for everybody as Deedy has told me, but it is always remarkable. As I leave, I tap on my communicator in my ear. "Heading back to the office, Gabby. Is there coffee?"

So that's my story and I'm sticking to it. The afterlife is a lot like the right-now life. You get out of it what you put into it. You can make it into heaven or you can make it into Hell. But it's up to you to make it. And stop measuring yourself with a different yardstick than you measure everyone else. Just remember:

Create Joy

Be indiscriminate with your kindness.

Forgive... Period... Even Yourself... Especially Yourself.

Love Unconditionally.

Understand that sometimes you might be the student, sometimes you might be the teacher, and sometimes, you just might be the lesson. But you were created by God to be exactly what you are. Never forget that.

Everything happens for a reason. God does not move you around like a chess piece micro-managing every detail in your life. But I believe that God does guide us on particular paths — even the ones where highwaymen are waiting to ambush us. There is something to be gained from every experience. Embrace that.

Stop thinking that you have all the answers. Whether it be in life, or in the afterlife. We each have a thread in a giant tapestry. Whether that thread is our religion, faith, morality, values, culture, or flaws, it is part of a greater tapestry. So weave it into others. Try to learn from them, as well as teach them. Because I think that if we could see that giant tapestry, we would be looking at God.

And most importantly, life is just a temp job. Ultimately it is one you're going to get fired from, at some point. So learn what you can, and have some fun, and stop taking yourself so damned seriously! And when they hand you your termination slip, don't forget to pack up all the love and good memories to take with you. Otherwise, you might end up in Hell. And trust me, waking up in Hell? Definitely NOT recommended.

Epitaph

This was a story. Just a story, about what I think it means to go to heaven or Hell. It's not an indictment on religion (any religion.) It's not intended to be sacrilegious or disrespectful. These are my words, and I thank my Creator (whoever he/she may turn out to be) for every single one of them. Even the approximate sixty three times when the word was the f-bomb. The one word that my mom is going to sigh over and tell me I should watch my language.

Speaking of Mom — I am one. My daughter Linda and my son Patch were a big part of writing this book and not just as inspiration. Those two little miracles even before either one of them could speak, taught me how to love unconditionally, so for that I will always be grateful for them and to them.

My father is a Methodist Minister, and I remember him telling a story from the pulpit when I was young. I've since heard it several more times from other people too, but I've always remembered it. It goes like this: There was once an an old man who knew he would die soon. He wanted to know what Heaven and Hell were like. He visited a wise man in his village to ask, "Can you tell me what Heaven and Hell are like?"

The wise man led him down a strange path, deep into the countryside. Finally they came upon a large house with many rooms and went inside.

Inside they found lots of people and many enormous tables with an incredible array of food.

Then the old man noticed a strange thing, the people, all thin and hungry were holding chopsticks 12-feet long. They tried to feed themselves, but of course could not get the food to their mouths with such long chopsticks.

The old man then said to the wise man "Now I know what Hell looks like, will you please show me what Heaven looks like?" The wise man led him down the same path a little further until they came upon another large house similar to the first. They went inside and saw many people well fed and happy, they too had chopsticks 12-feet long. This puzzled the old man and he asked, "I see all of these people have

12-foot chopsticks too, yet they are well fed and happy, please explain this to me.

The wise man replied, "in Heaven we feed each other"

I think that story, combined with all the lessons that I have (unfortunately) been determined to learn the hard way during this life, is what became the stock for the soup that turned into this. I hope it fed someone   out   there.

I'd like to thank every person in my life who gave me a reason to smile, a reason to cry, a reason to forgive, and a reason to be forgiven.

And thank you. Writing something doesn't mean shit. It has to be read before it can be a book.

-Helen Downing

ABOUT THE AUTHOR

Helen Downing has aspired to be many things in life. An actress, a writer, a trophy wife, a publicist, and a bang up media sales executive. In reality, she's a chubby, middle-aged, twice-divorced battleaxe who is addicted to sci-fi and social networking.

Please buy this book. It's her only chance of ever fulfilling her full potential, and possibly getting into heaven.

Follow Helen on Twitter: @imtellinhelen

16141082R00121

Made in the USA
Charleston, SC
06 December 2012